Romance ...
is that what makes us
fall in love?

Or, is it falling in love
that makes everything
romantic?

Come ... rediscover romance
and fall in love ...
with Ponder Romance.

AUTUMN'S EVE

JORDANNA BOSTON

A Ponder Romance

Published by Ponder Publishing Inc.

Autumn's Eve

A Ponder Romance Book
Published by Ponder Publishing Inc.
P.O. Box 23037 RPO McGillivray
Winnipeg, Manitoba
R3T 5S3 Canada

U.S. Address: 60 East 42nd Street, Suite 1166, New York, New York, 101655
Internet address: http://www.ponderpublishing.com

Canadian Cataloguing in Publication Data

Boston, Jordanna, 1963-
Autumn's eve

ISBN 0-9681587-1-4

I Title

PS8553 07399A88 1998 C813' 54 C98-900595-X
PR9199 3 B68A88 1998

Cover Photography: D. Lemke
Cover Design: PeR Design

ISBN 0-9681587-1-4

Printed in Canada

ONE

Eve kicked the door to the cold-room closed and dragged the sack of potatoes out of the kitchen and into the restaurant, where it was just a little more interesting to peel them. She slumped the sack against a wall and sank into a vinyl chair, drinking in the setting sun which, despite its long beams of light, was not quite able to polish the old arborite tables and tiled restaurant floor.

Reaching into the sack, she pulled out a wrinkled potato and began peeling, occasionally sparing a glance out the window to the creek which ran through the backyard. Some days a fox or even a bear would mosey along, and there was always an assortment of birds flitting about. Often she would spot a muskrat or beaver in the water, and every once in a while a deer ventured beyond the bush and into her view.

Once or twice she looked in the direction of the highway out front and the dirt road which intersected it, wishing a vehicle might happen along. The local folk almost always stopped in for a cup of coffee and a short visit when driving by. Everyone seemed to know Eve found it lonesome ever since Jake had moved out.

If she didn't recognize the driver, and the car didn't pull in for gas, she could at least pass the time guessing what purpose might bring a stranger past Jake's Corner, although few travellers ever drove by the *Last Chance Gas and Grill* without stopping. It really was the last chance for gas and food for the next two-hundred kilometres north to Foster Rapids, Manitoba, a small and decaying mining community.

But this late afternoon, as Eve quietly peeled potatoes and the sun inched its way behind the horizon, no vehicles passed, no animals paused to lap at the creek ... even the birds seemed noticeably absent. The silence was almost ominous, as though announcing even nature itself was abandoning Jake's Corner.

She dropped another potato into the pail of water on the floor beside her and wiped a splatter of water from her cheek with the back of her hand. How long before Jake's Corner was nothing more than mere memories in photo albums? She knew nobody blamed her, but she couldn't help but feel responsible. Her attempt to save the community had ended up sealing its eventual death. How could she have known? Perhaps if her head hadn't been so full of dreams ...

She picked up another potato and began carving out the eyes which had stubbornly sprouted, marvelling that something as good as dead could still grow. She stared at it thoughtfully for a long moment. She had to believe.

* * *

Dane Newson rubbed his eyes and tried once more to stretch out the stiffness which had slowly crept over his solid frame. The truck hit another pothole and jarred him sharply. He gritted his teeth as he manoeuvred the luxury passenger truck around another gaping hole in the gravel road. It might be a four-wheel-drive with an off-road suspension, but he couldn't imagine any vehicle riding smoothly on *this*. He couldn't believe they actually called it a highway.

He glanced at the clock on the dash and looked out over the horizon. It would be dark soon, and Foster Rapids was still more than two hours away. He probably should have checked in at a motel back in Thompson, but he hadn't anticipated the drive being so miserable.

This was as far north as he'd ever been, and while he didn't mind that, he certainly minded the road. Or highway, as the provincial road signs insisted upon calling it. A miserable, winding, twisting and lumpy piece of work, with nothing to look at but rocks and trees and the occasional lake. The Canadian Shield at its best. If it weren't for the First Nations Reservations he passed every now and then, he'd have felt starkly isolated.

He grimaced darkly. Maybe he should have just let his research team do what they do best. Part of the reason his business, Newson Enterprises, was so successful was due to the extensive research and scrutiny prospective investments were subjected to, long before he even considered sinking money into them. And although he seemed to know intuitively which ventures would make money just by looking at them, he didn't normally travel to a site until much later in the investigation. And he certainly didn't drive, not this far anyway.

The truck continued to whip past one boring stretch of landscape after another, and he couldn't help but chuckle. He had flown from Toronto to

Winnipeg and from there, instead of chartering a plane, had embarked on this road trip simply because he had wanted time to think and clear his head. Apparently, his wish had been granted since nothing around him could even remotely capture his attention.

The truck rounded another bend and a dilapidated-looking gas station came into view. *Last Chance Gas & Grill,* a faded and tattered sign announced as it clung forlornly to the side of the building. He'd better fill up and stretch his legs. Maybe he'd grab a coffee and a sandwich before continuing on. He could only guess what awaited him in Foster Rapids, Manitoba.

* * *

With one final burst of fire, the sunset lavishly bathed the forest in brilliant hues of orange and red, making an already opulent display of autumn colours nearly as outstanding as the sunset itself. Eve was so lost in it she didn't notice the black vehicle slowly etching its way across the colour-splashed canvas until it was nearly at Jake's Corner. She watched the truck slow as it approached, as if the driver were deliberating whether or not to stop, but in the end he heeded the warning of the sign outside — *next stop 200 kms overtop a crossed out 125 miles* — and pulled in, stopping at the gas pump.

Happy for the diversion, Eve dropped the potato peeler and hurried to the door, slamming the screen door behind her as she stepped outside and strode towards the pumps. The truck door opened and out climbed six feet of solid rock wearing a man's body, silk shirt, casual slacks and expensive shoes.

Eve stopped and stared. There hadn't been a man

like him around here for a long, long time. His hair, a streaky mixture of honey blond and brown, was short and wavy and flecked with grey at his temples. A day's growth of whiskers shadowed his cheeks and chin.

Her heart nearly stopped beating when he raised green eyes to hers. Maybe there was a hint of grey in them, too, or maybe it was just the way he was looking at her.

"I need a fill, and if the restaurant's still open, I wouldn't mind a coffee and a sandwich," he said with a tight smile which betrayed road weariness.

He has dimples! Eve nearly giggled as she walked around the vehicle, turned on the pump and opened the vehicle's gas cap. "Chicken," she said as she locked the gas nozzle in place and began wiping the windshield.

"Pardon me?"

She walked around to the other side of the windshield. "I only have chicken to make a sandwich with, if that's all right."

"That would be just fine," he replied.

Eve liked the sound of his voice. Deep and smooth. She glanced up at him and immediately wished she hadn't. He'd been staring at her belly which her brief tank top and jeans fell short of covering.

Her knees weakened momentarily. It wasn't as if a man staring at her was so unusual. She knew she'd been put together well and even liked to dress in a way that showed it all off. Someone had to spice up the lives of the men out here, since there were so few women around. Of course, she'd had her share of amorous lads and wild drunks to deal with, but for the most part, the local men simply appreciated the view.

But this stranger's gaze was different. It made her jeans feel skin tight and her belly exposed. She finished wiping the rear window and replaced the brush in the pail. Okay, so her jeans *were* skin tight and her belly *was* exposed. She just wasn't usually aware of it. Not that it bothered her; she simply wasn't sure what to do about it.

She tucked her chin-length, chestnut hair behind an ear and gave him a half-smile. "C'mon in, and I'll make a fresh pot of coffee."

He fell into step beside her as she climbed back up the steps to the store.

"Is the highway always that rough?" he asked, pausing to open the door for her.

Eve couldn't help but laugh. "Officially, it's Provincial Highway four hundred and six, but we call it *The Gauntlet.*"

His green eyes danced with amusement. "You people should make it a tourist attraction and charge a toll. It's the ride of a lifetime."

"You haven't even gotten to the best part yet!" Eve laughed again as she led him to a table in the small restaurant.

His look of surprise was genuine. "You mean it gets worse?"

Eve grabbed the stale coffee from the burner and dumped it down the drain. "Fraid so!" She switched on the machine. "It's never been well maintained. Not even when the mine was in full operation. I suppose it's because Foster Rapids is the end of the line. It's pretty much by foot or canoe after that."

He sat down at a table and grimaced. "Sounds like the highway from hell."

Eve laughed softly. She almost felt sorry for him. He was exhausted and quite obviously from the big city. Her guess was Toronto. Winnipeggers knew what to expect from Manitoba's country roads because their city ones weren't much better. The climate extremes — hot, dry summers and long, brutally cold winters — made them difficult, as well as expensive, to keep up. "Help yourself when it's ready," she told him before heading into the kitchen.

* * *

Dane watched her walk away. That was one hot little number, and she knew it, too. If the way she dressed didn't tell you, then the bold way she looked at you did. This was no shrinking violet. He'd bet she had all the local men tied up in knots. She was a wild one, all right. He hadn't noticed a ring but felt sorry for the poor soul who might be unfortunate enough to actually try and tie her down someday.

He grinned. She wasn't his type, he liked them much more sophisticated, but wild did have a certain appeal.

He got up and went to the coffee maker, not at all surprised to find the standard white mugs, which every diner seemed to use, waiting on a tray beside a basket of sugar cubes. He poured a coffee, dropped in some sugar, but passed on the cream when he noticed a ring around the rim of the creamer, suggesting it had been sitting out of the refrigerator too long.

He could hear her humming in the kitchen as she worked. He couldn't imagine what sort of chicken sandwich required all the chopping, sizzling and banging. He'd been in enough small towns over the years to know that a chicken sandwich was pretty standard fare. Two pieces of white bread, mayonnaise, lettuce and a slice or two of chicken breast. He even knew enough not to bother with a *hold the mayo* since it seemed to come with it on anyway, and if you dared to bring it to the attention of the waitress, the whole restaurant turned to stare at you as if you were from another planet.

* * *

The sun had gone down when Eve set the plate in front of him. She could tell he hadn't expected grilled chicken breast on a freshly baked roll. She'd faintly sprinkled it with fresh tarragon from the herb garden in the kitchen window and served it with a few fresh, raw vegetables. She was a good cook.

She seated herself at an opposite table and continued peeling potatoes, often looking at him while she worked, waiting for conversation. He didn't say anything. He simply cut through his sandwich and turned back to the newspaper he'd taken from the stack at the cash register. She suspected his sudden seeming oblivion to her was merely his city way. Had she been at Jake's Corner so long that it seemed odd when a stranger kept to himself?

She'd come a long way since Bryce and her years in Toronto. She was startled that the thought of him was still sickening to her and was reminded of him now simply because both Bryce and this stranger exuded an aura of money that could come only from Toronto. It was the expensive but conservative clothes and up-to-date but discreet haircut; the brand-new, rented luxury four-wheel-drive; the slight, polished, Eastern-Canadian accent, and the unstated expectation that he be given the best and treated with deference. She'd eat her socks if he didn't work on Bay Street. She wondered if he was married. He didn't seem the type. Married men had a completely different air about them. You could always pick them out.

"You're from Toronto?" she asked at last, when she could stand the silence no longer.

He lifted his head and stared at her in amazement. "Is it that obvious?"

Eve smiled slowly and paused to drop another potato into the pail of water. "Well, I guess ... maybe."

"Why wouldn't you have guessed some other city?"

"I lived there for awhile."

His grin made his dimples come alive. "That would explain the fancy sandwich." He put down his fork and sipped at his coffee and grinned again. "Is it on the menu or did you make it specifically for me?"

He was flirting with her.

"It's on the menu," she lied. "It says *Fancy Chicken Sandwich.*"

"Does it now?" He retrieved the laminated menu from behind the napkin holder and read it silently. "Ah, yes. Here it is. *Fancy Chicken Sandwich for Strangers from Toronto.*"

Eve let herself grin back at him. She supposed he wasn't all that bad. She could maybe even like him if he weren't so citified. She shuddered inwardly. Life with Bryce had cured her of ever wanting to live in any city again, or with any city man again, especially one from Toronto.

His green eyes twinkled merrily. "So do all strangers get preferential treatment, or just the ones from Toronto?"

Eve cocked her head to one side and smiled slyly. "It all depends."

"On what?"

"On whether I like the person or not and whether or not I think he or she will appreciate it."

He was incredulous. "Do you mean that a person might come in here and order ham and eggs and end up with *Eggs Benedict?*"

"It's possible."

He chuckled. "Doesn't anyone get upset?"

"Did you?"

"No, I guess I didn't." He grinned. "But why not just give people what's on the menu?"

"It gets a little boring out here by myself, serving the same old stuff all the time," she said as she dropped the last potato into the pail and began cleaning up the peelings. "Besides, most customers like the change, too. People around here know my menu is just a guideline." She dragged the pail of potatoes towards the kitchen, slopping water as she went. "However, on your way back from Foster Rapids, I can always serve you a boring chicken sandwich with plenty of mayonnaise."

"And what makes you so sure I'll stop in on my way back?" he asked, green eyes laughing.

Eve slid him a slow grin before she disappeared through the kitchen door. "Everybody does."

TWO

Dane was still grinning to himself as he climbed back into the truck and wiped his rain-soaked forehead before steering the truck onto the highway and into the steady downpour.

She sure was a charmer. Eve, she had said her name was. Eve what? he had asked, almost demanded, as he had paid his bill. Just Eve, she had replied simply.

He chuckled and shifted into four-wheel-drive to accommodate what was now a furious deluge mashing the road into a slippery combination of mud and gravel. Immediately he felt the tires beneath him gain a stronger grip.

No doubt, everyone did indeed return to her restaurant. And it likely wasn't for her cooking, which, he had to admit, wasn't all that bad. Who would ever expect to find a treat like her way out here? It had been difficult to keep his eyes off that firm, bare abdomen. Bellybuttons didn't usually do much for him, but hers certainly seemed to. And it had been almost impossible to keep his eyes from straying to and lingering on the generous swell trapped behind her tight little top.

The truck went into a skid, swerving his thoughts

back to the road. She had cautioned him against driving to Foster Rapids tonight after it had started to rain. She had even offered to put him up for the night, in one of the spare rooms, rather than see him risk the drive.

He had refused, partially because he was due back in Toronto in a few days. The few hours he would save by arriving tonight would enable him to do an extensive investigation into the property in which he was considering investing. The other reason was that he wasn't sure he could trust himself around her.

She might like to flirt, but he had the distinct impression casual sex was out of the question. Always. And it made him feel even more reckless around her. In fact, it was the very innocence of her offer that had made him refuse, as if the thought of anything else had never entered her head. She was simply being hospitable. Not only was it a shocking contrast to the cutthroat corporate jungle he hacked his way through on a daily basis, but it was so alluring that he couldn't trust himself not to selfishly coax it away from her.

"I feel like I'm sending you to your death," Eve had said as he had paid for the gas and sandwich. "Last year an entire family was killed in weather like this, and they were locals. They knew the road."

"I appreciate your concern," Dane had said, "but I'm facing a busy day in Foster Rapids tomorrow."

"If you're shy about staying here, don't be. People often stay upstairs, rather than risk being stranded on *The Gauntlet.*"

He had looked into those grave, brown eyes, knowing he'd probably be safer fighting the weather than fighting himself.

A crack of lightning, followed by a roar of thunder, interrupted his thoughts and revealed a massive figure in the middle of the road ahead. Bright eyes slowly turned to face his headlights which illuminated an enormous moose. Instinctively, Dane slammed on the brakes and swerved. Hitting that moose would kill him; he might at least stand a chance of surviving in the ditch.

The truck lost its grip in the thick gumbo and slid into the ditch on a sharp angle. Dane knew it was going to roll. Nevertheless, he tried vainly to regain control. Over the truck went. His briefcase and cellular phone whizzed past his head. The last thing he saw was his luggage coming at him from somewhere in the back.

* * *

Eve wiped down the stainless steel counter and turned off the lights in the kitchen and restaurant. She usually left one on in the store and at the gas pumps just to let travellers know help was available if needed. An explosive smash of thunder shook the old building, making her half-wonder if it wouldn't fall down around her one of these years. She peered out a rain-soaked window into the black night and wondered how the stranger from Toronto was doing. Dane Newson, he had said his name was.

Remembering the invitation in those green eyes, Eve grinned as she went to the cash register, stuffed the float into one envelope and the day's cash and receipts into another and dropped both down the safe chute; he'd be back, if only to see what she'd serve him. She leaned on the display case and studied the chocolate bars. That is, if he makes it to Foster Rapids in the first place.

She couldn't shake the ominous feeling that had come upon her, nor could she keep her mind off the

Morrisette family. It had been a night such as this when their car had skidded sideways into a tree, killing all four of them. Eve had been the last person to see them alive.

She clicked the front door deadbolt into place and peered out the window one last time. Jake sometimes came by in bad weather just to make sure she was all right. Maybe she would ask him to drive a little way down the highway to look for Dane Newson. It wouldn't be the first time he'd gone in search of someone. Emergency help was virtually nonexistent in isolated places like Jake's Corner. People had to look out for each other as best they could, and Jake's monster of a vehicle was more like a tank than a truck, even though it was so old it was almost prehistoric.

Eve assumed it must have started out as a tractor, but over the years he had modified it into what he believed was the truest form of an all-terrain-vehicle in existence. It was so outlandish the province wouldn't permit him a license for it. But, Jake, never one to surrender to authority, drove it anyway. The local RCMP detachment had long ago stopped issuing tickets, or threatening to impound it, since they themselves had, from time to time, enlisted the help of Jake's vehicle for rescue missions.

Eve sighed deeply. She felt silly for worrying. She turned out the light and headed up the back stairs. Jake wouldn't think she was being silly. He knew how deeply the Morrisettes' death had affected her.

* * *

Dane ignored the frigid rain pouring down upon him and leaned against the upside down truck, trying to catch his breath. Crawling out had been hard work. The door was jammed, so he had to roll down the window and squeeze himself through it. Unbuckling his seatbelt had proven impossible. Fortunately, he always kept a small pocketknife on him — a habit from his boyhood. However, sawing through a seatbelt with a pocket knife was more of a task than he had guessed, especially when hanging upside down.

His head throbbed, although he didn't think he had been unconscious for very long. According to his watch, he'd only left the *Gas and Grill* about a half-hour ago. He calculated that it was approximately a ten-kilometre walk back.

He looked heavenward. Lightning cracked almost continuously while thunder roared in response. It was beginning to look as if he might never get to Foster Rapids, let alone by tomorrow. He reached down inside the window of the truck, scooped up his cellular phone, which needed to be recharged, and then started the slippery ascent out of the ditch. He had a feeling it was going to be a long night.

He stood shivering at the roadside a moment. He hadn't encountered a single vehicle the entire time he'd been driving. Obviously, he would either have to seek the shelter of his overturned truck, with the slim hope someone might drive by, or start walking. He pulled the collar of his leather jacket close about him and looked down the road. Except for the flashes of lightning, it was pitch black. He knew the truck had gone into the ditch on the right, so he felt certain of the direction he needed to go, but otherwise he was walking almost completely blind. At least the road was still reasonably firm beneath him. As long as he stayed out of the trees, he would end up back at Eve's sooner or later.

He wouldn't permit himself to dwell on how likely

it was to be later than sooner, if ever. He was cold. Too damn cold to think about anything, and it was some time before he realized he'd been wrapping himself in thoughts of Eve. Her warm restaurant, her warm dark eyes with their long sweep of delicate lashes ...

It occurred to him that he had never thought of Vanessa in such a way, of running to her for comfort. He remembered the feel of her skin. It was cold. Vanessa was always cold. She hated the damp Toronto winters and often whined about how they should move somewhere warm like Florida. "It's not as if you can't do business down there just as well," she'd sniff.

The raven-haired beauty had been making noises about marriage for months and had given him an ultimatum a few weeks back. He hadn't seen any reason to alter their situation. The sex was great. They had toothbrushes in each other's bathrooms and clothes hanging in each other's closets. When he needed a hostess, or a date, she was usually available and always performed her role to perfection. She had a brain, too. And she didn't bore him the way many women eventually did.

He supposed he couldn't really blame her for wanting more, but neither would he pretend that he could give it. And so here he was, alone — *literally*, he thought with derision as he blinked into the drowning blackness ahead — trying to figure out why, if he'd made the right decision, did his life suddenly seem so ... he wasn't even sure *empty* described it.

He had to admit that, to some degree, Vanessa was right in insisting it was time he settled down. He was at the tail end of his thirties. What more was he waiting for? He'd already conquered most of the goals he'd set for himself, both professionally and personally; he'd amassed enough wealth to never need work again, should he so choose, and despite all his success, his business could still give him an adrenalin rush. Was this what the rest of his days would consist of? Chasing down the next thrill or kill?

He stomped the water out of his shoes and bent down to tie them tighter, laughing as he realized nothing could keep the rain out. It occurred to him that at least he could laugh. Vanessa didn't know how. Perhaps, he surmised, as he continued to forge through the rain, it was one of the reasons he'd never grown to love her, at least not the way a woman needed to be loved. The closest their relationship had ever come to love was *comfortable*, and even though she would have easily settled for that and the little bit of love he could give her, the thought of spending the rest of his days with her ... maybe he was the one who wanted more. Maybe he was the one who expected too much. Would life with someone you didn't love be better than life alone?

And what was love anyway? It's not like he'd seen much of it. Did any couple actually love each other the way they claimed to? All the married guys he knew, with the exception of his business partner, Nelson Adsum, all either cheated on their wives or eventually divorced them. Even his old man had traded in his mother for a younger model, and although he'd eventually come to forgive his father for the destruction he'd caused, it was something he'd vowed never to do himself — not to Vanessa, not to any woman, and certainly not to his children. It was one of the reasons he'd said no to Vanessa. How could he enter into such an agreement with a woman he didn't love? He laughed derisively.

Unless he wanted to spend the rest of his life alone, it seemed his only option was to find a woman he did love.

Dane grimaced as he continued to trudge along, the rain pelting at him so hard that it forced him to walk with his eyes closed, the fleeting moments the wind let up providing little relief since the water then merely rushed down his hair and into his eyes. He just wanted to get warm and dry.

His thoughts found their way to Eve again, and eventually he stopped noticing how the water in his shoes gushed out with every step, or that absolutely every inch of him was soaked and frozen. What was she doing out here? She didn't belong. She belonged in a mansion and elegant evening dresses, and the irrepressible grace beneath that sassy exterior told him she'd once known both.

And yet ... she seemed so at home at the *Last Chance*, as though it had been erected solely for her. She appears, and suddenly one forgets how dilapidated and forlorn the place is; she smiles and one is immediately blinded; she looks deep into your eyes and you're entranced.

Dane stumbled over a rock in the dark and grinned in self-deprecation. Either he'd been hit on the head harder than he'd thought, or she'd cast some sort of spell over him.

He laughed out loud. He'd be spouting poetry next. Luckily, he didn't know any. Oh well, if he was going to die of hypothermia out here on this lonely stretch of road in the middle of a rainstorm, he might as well indulge in a few fantasies. They'd find him face down in the mud, smiling like an idiot!

He was still stumbling along, thinking about Eve, when a half-dozen yellow lights appeared in front of him, and the most bizarre vehicle he'd ever seen stopped in the middle of the road, nearly blinding him with its glare of lights.

"Get in!" a voice barked from inside as the vehicle noisily rolled closer.

Dane walked around to what he assumed would be the passenger's side and pulled on what looked like a door handle. The door gave way and he climbed up into the cab.

The driver was an ancient man of an indeterminate age. His slight build appeared frail, and his skin was weather-beaten and fiercely wrinkled. On his head was a weary old cap which advertised a brand of motor oil and from under which thin wisps of white hair clung desperately to his neck.

"Thanks," Dane said, extending his hand. "My truck rolled in the ditch a few kilometres back. I had pretty much given up hope of anyone coming along."

The old man ignored Dane's extended hand and without so much as a grunt, turned the vehicle back to the direction from which it had come.

Dane wrenched his head around. He had assumed they would drive to his truck. "Would you mind driving me to my truck?" he asked. "It's not too far, and winching it upright shouldn't be too much trouble."

"I ain't doin' nothin' in this weather," the old man grumbled, turning the fan on so high it almost drowned out the sound of his voice as it blasted tornadoes of heat every which way. Despite the welcome warmth, Dane turned away to hide his amusement and smiled into the wet darkness slapping against his window.

"My cell phone needs to be recharged," Dane said some moments later in another attempt at conversation. "Perhaps I could call for a tow truck from the *Gas and Grill* if it's still open."

"Phone's out."

Of course. What was with this guy? He again extended his hand. "Dane Newson. Newson Enterprises."

"Jake," the old fellow replied tersely, tightening his grip on the wheel.

"No last name?"

"Jake's fine."

Just Jake ... just Eve. It dawned on him. "Eve sent you?"

The old guy grunted what Dane assumed must have been a *yes* and tossed a stainless-steel thermos at him. It was full of hot coffee. Dane poured some into the lid and offered it to Jake.

"Don't take it with that stuff," he growled.

Dane assumed he meant the cream and sugar. He took a sip, and it warmed him all the way down. She had put some whiskey in it. "She's something, isn't she?" he said. "What a surprise to find a piece of work like her out here."

The glare Jake gave him was downright frightening. And did he hear a snarl? Dane took a deep swig of coffee and quickly changed the subject. "I'm surprised that my vehicle rolled so easily." The old man cast him a disapproving scowl which clearly implied he thought Dane's accident was completely unrelated to the vehicle and entirely the fault of his driving.

He supposed the old man was right. He lived in a condominium along Lake Ontario, just blocks from his office. He jogged the distance every morning and, twice a week, followed it up with a two-hour workout at the gym on the top floor of the office building. He seldom drove his BMW, unless he was taking clients golfing or out of the downtown area, and he preferred limousine service to hunting down a parking space.

"Dang?" the old man asked. "That Korean?"

"Excuse me?"

"Sounds Korean."

"What does?"

"Dang."

Dane grinned. The old man thought his name was Dang. "No, it's D-A-N-E, Dane."

The old man shifted gears. "I was too old to fight in that war. I was in World War II. I went over a boy and came back a man." His glare insinuated a man was never a man until he'd fought in a war.

Dane's smile was congenial. "I own an investment company. I guess I have people like yourself to thank for the freedom which allows it to survive." That should placate the old goat, he thought moodily.

The old man shifted in his seat and mumbled a "hmpf." His scowl deepened.

Dane sighed audibly. He'd try one more time. "I was on my way to Foster Rapids. I'm considering investing in a new lodge at Lake of the Wolves. I think the North presents a great deal of economic potential if it's developed correctly."

The old man said nothing as he continued to stare through the sheet of rain that obscured the road in front of him.

It was going to be a long drive back to the *Last Chance Gas and Grill.*

"Enterprises?" The old guy's glare was demanding. "What's that? It don't sound like work."

Dane suppressed a scowl of his own. "I suppose you might say it's a way of making your money work for you."

"Just like I thought ... it ain't work."

"Actually, it's a lot of work. I spend a great deal of time looking for, and investigating, businesses which are seeking financial backers. When I find one which I think could benefit from my financial assistance, and more importantly, one which will most likely be successful, I arrange to purchase the company, in whole or in part. More often than not, I end up working very closely with the new business, helping to ensure that it is a success."

"Call it work if you want," Jake grumbled testily, "still sounds like you're a bum to me."

Dane groaned inwardly. Perhaps it was best to pass the time in silence since it was quite obvious that nothing he did would meet with Jake's approval. Apparently, Jake was of the same mind as Dane because he said no more and merely stared out the windshield.

The sight of the gas station pumps as the truck rounded a corner brought a swell of relief. Dane strained to see the glow of yellow light pouring into the night through the store windows, hoping for a glimpse of Eve. A fork of lightning punctuated her sudden appearance, and he found himself pondering the electricity that shot through him at the sight of her.

"You married?" the old guy asked, pulling the vehicle to a halt. It sounded more like an attack than a question.

"No."

"Thought so," the old guy growled as he pushed his door open and climbed out.

The door of the *Last Chance* swung open, and Eve stepped out and stood under the awning, bath towels and blankets in hand.

"He's soaked right through and cranky as all get out," Jake bellowed at her through the curtain of rain, "but he'll live."

* * *

Eve had heard Jake's truck before she'd seen it. She'd been doing a crossword puzzle to help pass the time when the vehicle rumbled and sputtered its way onto the lot, belching in protest one last time in front of the gas pumps as Jake cut the engine. Her relief that Dane was with him and appeared to be okay was tempered with distress that her premonition had been correct.

Jake shuffled into the store, followed by a severely wet Dane Newson. "His truck ain't doin' too good."

Dane grinned sheepishly, towelling his hair dry. "I rolled it."

"You rolled a four-by-four?" Eve's smile was incredulous.

He slung the towel around his neck and followed her into the restaurant. "Yes, apparently it's quite an accomplishment." He peeled off his sopping jacket and wrapping a blanket around himself, sank into a chair. Jake silently settled into a chair at an opposite table.

"It is!" Eve affirmed as she poured them both coffee. "But fortunately, you seem to have come through it in one piece."

Dane gave her a deep smile. "Whatever possessed you to send him looking for me?"

Eve couldn't resist a grin as she passed him the coffee and pointed to the sign above the gas pumps. "The sign does say *Full Service.*"

"Really?" Dane grinned back, dimples dancing. "All that for the price of a tank of gas? What service comes with the guest room?"

Eve suspected his mild flirtation was motivated more by curiosity than true interest, but she enjoyed flirting every now and then. She raised an eyebrow.

"That all depends on the guest."

Jake shifted in his seat, scraping his chair in noisy disapproval. "You don't look Korean."

Dane turned to him, his irritation well under control. "No, it's Dane, like someone from Denmark. D-A-N-E."

"I was in Europe during the war. I didn't hear of no Danish folks by the name of Dang."

Eve couldn't help but feel sympathy for Dane. Jake was being deliberately obtuse and unusually cantankerous, all in an effort to intimidate him. She knew it was Jake's way of protecting her. "Try Dan," she mouthed overtop of her coffee mug.

Dane winked a *thank-you.* "Why don't you just call me Dan?" he suggested pleasantly.

"What you call yourself is all the same to me," Jake replied as he drained the last of his coffee,"-cept a fellow shouldn't be ashamed of the name his mother give him. I don't mind callin' ya Dang."

Eve giggled into her coffee at Dane's suppressed groan. Jake wasn't about to be won over easily. "No, please, I would be happy if you just called me Dan."

Jake pushed out his chair, put on his cap and stood up. "Well, like I said, it's all the same to me."

Eve got up from her chair and going over to him, planted a kiss on his wrinkled cheek. "Thanks, Jake, for putting my mind at ease."

"What're ya kissin' me for?" Jake grumbled, but his frail arm went around her waist.

"I'll call Stanley in the morning and get him to winch out Mr. Newson's truck," she said.

"Tomorrow's Sunday," Jake replied dourly as he opened the front door. "Folks is supposed to go to church. If Dang there needs to have his truck before Monday, he'll have to call the rental company."

Through the restaurant window, Eve watched him

shuffle towards his truck. To her knowledge, Jake had been to church only twice in his life: once to get married and once to bury Mrs. Jake, and he had little use for folk who went more often than that. This sudden consideration for Sunday was peculiar. He must have taken an immediate and intense dislike to Dane. "Did you upset him in some way?" she asked Dane cautiously as she returned to the restaurant.

Dane's face was sheer surprise. "No, not at all. I swear," he said, his hands raised in protest. "He was grouchy right from the moment he found me. He told me to get in, practically threw the thermos of coffee at me and refused to shake hands. He barely said two words to me, except to hint that because you put whiskey in the coffee, I might have a drinking problem, or that I wasn't a man yet because I haven't served in a war."

"Hmm ..." Eve murmured as she traced a finger over a coffee ring on the table, "it's so unlike him."

"Maybe he was annoyed at having to come out in this weather," Dane suggested.

"No, he often goes out to rescue people. I even think he's glad for the opportunity to bring out *Sweet-Pea*."

"*Sweet-Pea*?" Dane laughed. "Is that what he calls that monstrosity?"

Eve nodded and grinned. "She's his baby. He spends hours and hours working on her."

"It figures," Dane chuckled. "A man that cranky would prefer the company of machines over humans."

She smiled slowly. "He pampers me pretty well. He'd give me the world if I asked."

Green eyes twinkled into hers. "I imagine plenty of men around here would give you the world if you asked for it."

Eve felt a tingle rise from her toes all the way to her fingers. He was flirting again. She studied his sandy hair, the sparkling sea in his eyes, and those dimples, and wondered how far she could safely flirt back before she found herself in too deep. And where exactly would too deep be? She let her eyes wander across his thick shoulders and wondered what his chest looked like without his shirt. A few fine hairs softly whispered over the last button. She liked a man with some hair on his chest.

Mentally, she slapped herself. What was she doing entertaining such thoughts? It was men like Dane Newson she had sought refuge from out here at Jake's Corner in the first place. The world was full of Dane Newsons.

"Yes, well," she said lightly, "none of them compare with sweet old Jake."

She could tell by the way he was looking at her that he had a fairly good idea what she'd been thinking. His grin deepened. "You've been in the bush too long if you think Jake is sweet!"

Eve put her hands on her hips and lectured him lightly. "He's really not that bad, and he's a better judge of character than you know because for as much as he pretends he doesn't like you, he'd have never left you alone with me if he truly thought you were a scoundrel."

Dane's burst of laughter filled the restaurant. "I don't know which to be more offended by — the fact that he refuses to call me by my name or that he's pegged me harmless enough to stay here unchaperoned."

Eve laughed with him but battled knots of apprehension inside. Dane might be harmless as far as Jake was concerned, but she sensed she was flirting with danger, not because she didn't trust

Dane, but because she didn't trust herself. Being in his presence was easy, comfortable, as if he belonged, right from the moment he'd stepped out of his rented truck. She'd better get rid of him pretty darn quick or she just might end up making a fool of herself over a man. Again.

THREE

The slamming of drawers, clanking of plates and banging of pots roused Dane. He opened his eyes and lay still for a moment with his hands behind his head, gathering his thoughts. He grinned. She sure was a boisterous cook. He wondered what she was concocting this time.

He let the blankets fall from his bare chest and sat up. He'd slept nude. He usually did. She'd tried to find him something to wear after he'd finally warmed up in a hot bath last night. He'd sat in the antique pedestal tub, with its chipped porcelain yellowed with years, thinking about how she would probably take a bath in it later. His mental picture hadn't quite matched the worn old tub. A creature like Eve belonged in a marble Jacuzzi with frothing water swirling about her smooth skin. He had run his hand along the edge of the tub, imagining her arm resting against it, and picked up the bar of soap from the little rack hanging over the edge. She'd probably use the same bar of soap, he had thought as he had dampened it, lathering it over his chest, the hair transforming the suds into a froth. He had imagined her running the soap over her smooth, silky skin. Her towel was probably the white one hanging on the rack by the closet ...

He pulled himself off the bed, reluctantly directing his thoughts away from forbidden places with Eve; the last thing he needed was his head in the clouds. In his business it was too easy to make serious errors with a distracted mind.

He chuckled as he recalled the embarrassment on her face when he had come out of the bathroom last night with only a towel wrapped around his waist. She had pressed her back against the wall, as if the hallway had become too small. Her reaction had surprised him. Instinct told him she was far from an innocent virgin, and the devil in him had made him prolong chatting with her for the sheer fun of watching her squirm.

"No luck finding dry clothes?"

"None that would be your size," she had said, her voice coming out in wispy breaths.

"I guess I'll have to sleep in the raw tonight," he had paused for emphasis, "but I can't very well wear a towel in the morning."

"I put your things in the wash. They should be dry by then."

She slipped by him, but he had followed her down the hall. "I guess you're used to this sort of thing."

She had difficulty keeping her eyes away from his chest. Women liked his chest. They liked running their fingers over the muscles through the spray of fine dark hairs. With feigned absentmindedness, he had scratched at his chest.

"What sort of thing?" she had asked, inching further back down the hall.

"Stranded folks sleeping naked in your guest rooms."

And then, suddenly, she had seemed to grasp that what he was doing was deliberate. Scratching his chest had been overkill. Her immediate transformation back into the confident woman she was had been a treat to behold. Her dark eyes had hooded seductively, her lips curling into a secretive smile, her brows arched.

"Maybe they don't always sleep in the guest rooms."

He chuckled again and tidied the bed covers, smoothing them over the slouching bed which was more comfortable than it looked, despite likely being older than Jake himself. He wondered if she'd made the polka-dot curtains and matching quilt and supposed that, at one time, they might have cheered the barren and tired-looking room but now, being patched and faded, only added to the room's sadness.

But then everything about the *Last Chance* was sad and tired. It depressed him. He could never live for long in a place like this. He wasn't the sort of man who needed a lot of amenities, but he liked a certain amount of brightness around him.

That's why Eve seemed so out of place. *She was the brightness out here.* He wondered, again, what had brought her here. Man troubles, he'd bet. It certainly wasn't the night life.

He grinned at the thought of what type of man captured her interest. Someone she could push around, likely. She seemed the type. He preferred his women more compliant than Eve.

He discovered his clothes, laundered and folded, on an antique chair near the door. He was mildly surprised. He was a light sleeper. She must have been extremely quiet, or he'd been sleeping with the dead.

He dressed and opened the door. The smell of bacon and eggs filled his nostrils. He was suddenly hungry. He supposed, as he started down the back staircase towards the kitchen, that he should call the rental agency and the people in Foster Rapids. Maybe he could arrange to have the truck put back on the road or hitch a ride somehow. He expelled a breath at the bottom of the stairs. At this moment, he didn't feel like doing any of those things.

He should probably call his office, too, and let them know he was okay. It occurred to him that it was the weekend and that the office would be closed. Still, odd as it was, he felt like he should call someone, as if he needed to hold onto something ... as if he were slipping away.

"Hey, sleepyhead!" Eve called out as she looked up from drizzling sauce over a plate of eggs.

"Eggs Benedict?" He laughed, itching to act on the impulse to wrap an arm around her waist and kiss her good morning like a besotted old husband. Yep, he was slipping away all right!

"Why not?" she said as she held a plate up to him. "You inspired me." She dropped the plate into his hands. "Would you mind running this out to Jake? I'm having trouble keeping everything co-ordinated."

She was wearing high heels and a miniskirt that was almost as tight as her scoop-necked tank top, which exposed nothing but certainly didn't hide anything either. Large hooped earrings hung about her neck. His eyes travelled downwards from the earrings. Jake would get out his rifle if he knew what he was thinking at this moment.

He took the plate from her. Their eyes met. The triumph in those brown depths was unmistakable. He chuckled as he headed towards the restaurant. The little vixen was paying him back for last night.

The grin fell from his face as he entered the restaurant. Every seat was filled, and almost everyone was either ninety, Native, or both. He'd never have suspected so many people lived in the vicinity, or that he'd be the odd man out.

Jake sat in a corner with two plump, elderly native women. He wound his way towards them through the legs and chairs filling the aisle.

"This here's Dang," Jake announced as Dane set the plate before him. "Some kind of Korean name, 'cept he likes to be called Dan, on account of being ashamed."

Before Dane could interject with his true name, the most elderly of the two women clasped his arm and said in a quivering voice, "Dang is a good name, your mother gave it to you," while her friend smiled and nodded her agreement.

Out of the corner of his eye, Dane caught a glimpse of malicious delight passing over Jake's withered face. The old codger had known all along exactly what his name was. What Dane could have done to earn the old man's undying animosity, he couldn't even begin to guess, nor would he bother to figure out. But he would beat the sour Jake at his own game, if not now, then before he left for Foster Rapids. He hadn't made Newson Enterprises into the success it was without knowing how to win.

He flashed the two women a dazzling smile. The kind of smile that made his dimples dance and his eyes sparkle. The kind of smile that had opened a lot more than doors when it came to women. "You're right, you make me think of my mother and I feel ashamed. I'd be honoured if you called me Dang."

Their response to his charm was instantaneous, and they beamed back at him approvingly. He slid a victorious glance towards Jake. That's when he noticed the man had no lower teeth. Jake was contentedly gumming his breakfast, apparently oblivious to everything but his food. Startled, Dane stared at him in shocked silence.

Jake raised his head, as if he suddenly remembered Dane's presence, and with an evil, toothless grin said, "You should try this here eggs, Dan. *Benedix* she calls them. They're dang good."

* * *

Eve watched Dane through the kitchen pickup window. She could see Jake was giving him a hard time again. She decided he deserved it after the way he had teased her last night. Her reaction to him as he had stepped out of the bathroom with only a towel between him and the breeze had taken her completely by surprise.

To see that mass of solid rock without clothes ... he must lift weights; the muscles were too perfectly formed to have been gained through manual labour. She had wanted to run her hands over them and feel them tense beneath her fingers ... just thinking about it almost made her dizzy.

Eve banged the fridge door shut and shook her head to expel the image. She had to pull herself together. She had clearly developed a case of bush fever. She needed to drive to the city and do some serious shopping and go dancing or something.

And as for Dane Newson, he had immediately picked up on her reaction to him, like any red-blooded male would have. But did he politely pretend not to notice? Absolutely not. Instead, he had chased her down the hall, affecting conversation, with the likely hope of her falling into his arms and maybe even his bed.

She dropped two plates of Eggs Benedict on the pickup counter as Dane came back. He'd pay for it, she'd see to it. He was already practically drooling at the sight of her in her miniskirt. She'd torment him by being as sexy as she knew how. Then she'd work him to death. He wouldn't know what hit him.

She gave him a bright smile and shoved the plates towards him. "Those two young fellows at the back — that's Gilbert Flett and Stanley Properzzi. Gilbert doesn't want any sauce."

Dane ignored the plates, leaned his arms on the counter and grinned. "Is this how you make your stranded guests pay their way?"

"Maybe ..." She lowered her eyes then brought them up to look deep into his. "Just exactly how are you planning to pay for it? Money doesn't mean a whole lot up here."

His dimples danced. "I'm sure I could think of some way to satisfy you."

Eve laughed and pointed a finger at him. "Now that would be a first!" She pushed the plates closer to him. "But in the meantime, I'll settle for having these delivered."

Dane picked up the plates of Eggs Benedict and shook his head mournfully. "You drive a hard bargain."

Eve shrugged. "Perhaps, but maybe I'm helping you, too. Stanley has a tow truck. Maybe you can convince him to help you out."

"Doesn't he have to go to church?" Mild sarcasm tinged his voice.

"Stanley already went to church."

Eve dropped more English muffins in the toaster and hurried back to watch Dane deliver Stanley and Gilbert their breakfast. They chatted seriously for a moment or two and then Dane returned.

"Well?"

"They called me Dan and said they don't work on the Lord's Day of Rest."

"What?" Eve couldn't believe it. Stanley and

Gilbert ran the local mechanics shop. Usually they were happy to have any kind of work, anytime of day or night, but there was no point in telling Dane that. He had troubles enough.

"They called you Dan?" She pulled the muffins from the toaster and arranged them on a plate. "Well, surely they're not hard of hearing. Maybe it's your Toronto accent."

"Torontonians don't have an accent."

"Yes they do. It's faint ... but your A's are longer. I could see someone mistaking Dane for Dang the way you say it." It was complete hogwash, but she didn't want to arouse Dane's suspicions. "It's sort of like the twang of the American south."

"I don't speak any differently than you."

"Sure you do. You should hear how your *any* just sounded."

Dane combed his hair with his hands in exasperation. "Look, are the phones working yet?"

Eve swallowed her surprise. "The phones?"

"Yes, the phones. Are they working now?"

"Uh ... probably." Where had he gotten the idea the phones weren't working?

"Do you mind if I use yours? I'll call collect."

Eve pointed to the telephone sitting by the cash register. "Be my guest."

While he tried to dial out, Eve grabbed two plates of Eggs Benedict and hurried out to Jake's table. "Why is everyone giving that man such a difficult time?"

Jake and his female companions stared up at her blankly then passed each other looks of confusion, but Eve wasn't buying their innocence. "Jake, you know darn well his name is Dane."

"Hey! Are those my eggs?" Andrew Cook called from the next table. "I don't want no cold breakfast."

Eve turned, dropped the plates in front of him and his wife and then went over to Stanley and Gilbert. "Why won't you help him out?" she asked quietly.

Gilbert, a handsome, twenty-something native man with long black hair and a big smile, leaned his chair back on two legs and grinned up at her. "It's Sunday. It's the Lord's Day of Rest."

"That's never stopped you before."

His white pal, Stanley, who was about the same age but much bigger and who sported red hair of the same length, also leaned back in his chair, his pale blue eyes mischievous. "The preacher preached a good sermon, and now we've realized the error of our ways. You don't want us to offend the Lord, do you?"

"Stanley, the only reason you went to church today was to see Crystal Desrosier's cousin who's visiting here from Brandon. Everyone knows you've been following her around like a lost puppy." Everyone in the restaurant guffawed loudly at Eve's comment and Stanley blushed a deep sheepish red. She leaned on the table. "Now, come on guys. The poor man is stranded."

Gilbert grinned again. "We'll be happy to help him out on Monday, after our day of rest."

Eve put her hands on her hips. "For your information, the Lord's Day of Rest is the Sabbath, which was yesterday, if you want to get technical about it! So you're a day late."

"Well, now," Gilbert was unperturbed, "us Christians like to honour God on Sundays. We'll be more than happy to lend a hand tomorrow."

Stanley punched his partner's arm playfully, his embarrassment subsided, and laughed. "Unless, of course, we're too busy Monday."

"You're supposed to fix my truck tomorrow,

remember Stanley?" Andrew Cook called out loudly.

"He better not," Bob Sanderson commented from the next table. "I've been waitin' three weeks for them to work on my hydraulic lift."

"See?" Gilbert said as he gestured helplessness with his hands. "We're pretty tied up tomorrow."

Eve sighed in resignation and returned to the kitchen.

"The phone is still out," Dane said when he emerged from the convenience store. His frustration showed plainly on his face. "That meeting in Foster Rapids is important."

"Mmm ... too bad," Eve replied, ignoring him while absently passing him another pair of plates. Weird things were happening at Jake's Corner this morning, and what could possibly be wrong with the phone?

He held a plate in each hand. "Where to now?"

"The table in front of Gilbert and Stanley — that's Mr. and Mrs. Epp. They usually drive to Foster Rapids on Sundays to visit their granddaughter and her children. Maybe they'll let you ride with them."

"At this point, I'm almost willing to walk rather than undergo being called Dang again."

Eve turned off the grill. "Oh no, not the Epps. They're much too polite. They'll not rest until they say it correctly. What I'd be worried about, if I were you, would be dying of boredom before they get you to Foster Rapids."

Dane dutifully delivered the plates to the Epps, and Eve slipped into the convenience store. She lifted the telephone receiver. It was definitely dead. She crouched down and opened the cupboard under the counter where the phone jack was located. It was definitely unplugged.

She peeked over the counter at Dane. Mrs. Epp

had him firmly by the arm and looked as if she had no intention of letting him go anytime soon. The Epps were a lonely elderly couple who had few people to talk to since the last of their children moved away several years ago, so when they had snagged someone to chat with, they didn't like to let go.

Eve closed the cupboard door and leaned on the counter top, trying to decide whether or not to plug the phone back in. It couldn't have become dislodged by accident, so obviously someone had wanted it unplugged. But why? And why was everybody acting so weird? Jake had everyone calling Dane *Dang*; Stanley and Gilbert had turned into churchgoers; and now the phone. She sighed. There was no rush to plug it in, except maybe for Dane's sake. She'd do it later. She wasn't sure she should interfere just yet with whatever was going on.

"They did call me Dane," he said when he came back, "but said their car is already full with goodies for their great-grandchildren —" He paused to grin. "About whom I now know everything from their school grades to which one hates peanut butter."

"You'd better not be in a hurry when the Epps get a hold of you!" Eve laughed, not surprised by now that they wouldn't take Dane to Foster Rapids. "What's so important about getting to Foster Rapids?" she asked him.

"I own an investment company," Dane explained. "We purchase large, usually controlling, shares in businesses needing financing. Businesses which we believe will return our investment with a healthy profit down the road."

"What on earth could there be worth investing in at Foster Rapids? It's almost as much of a ghost town as Jake's Corner."

"That's what you call this place?"

"What, Jake's Corner?"

"Yes."

"Of course. What did you think it was called?"

"I thought it was the *Last Chance Gas and Grill.*"

"This building is, but it's on Jake's Corner. The crossroad out there is called Jake's Road."

"The Jake who all of this is named after wouldn't happen to be that Jake out there? The crotchety old codger who snarls at me all the time?"

Eve had to laugh. "The one and only."

"So who owns the *Last Chance*?"

"Jake."

"Figures."

Eve passed him a serving of Eggs Benedict and a fork, and picking up her own plate, climbed onto an old chrome bar stool near the herb-garden window. She watched him watch her cross her legs. He found a wooden crate and settled down to eat his breakfast.

"Is your business successful?" Eve asked between mouthfuls.

"Very," Dane replied as he held up his fork.

"So, what's Foster Rapids got that Jake's Corner hasn't?"

He was eating with definite pleasure. "A potential hunting and fishing lodge for overseas tourists."

Eve swallowed her mouthful heavily, a sense of foreboding washing over her. "Where exactly would this lodge be?"

"A place called Lake of the Wolves. Do you know it?"

Eve's stomach curdled. Did she know it? They were practically sitting on it, and she owned over half the property along it. "Yes, fairly well."

"From the photographs I've seen, it's quite secluded and beautiful."

"Mmm ... yes it is," she mumbled absently, afraid of what the answer to her next question might be. "Who is building this new lodge?"

"A guy by the name of Frank Loewen. Do you know him?"

"Sort of." Eve felt sick. The lodge at Lake of the Wolves was her dream. Hers and Stanley and Gilbert's. And it was half-built. It would have been finished by now if a potential environmental hazard hadn't been anonymously brought to the provincial government's attention. The concern proved to be utterly groundless, but by the time they had paid for all the necessary studies and passed all the requirements, they had not only run out of the money they had borrowed but had also lost a summer's worth of potential and desperately needed revenue.

She knew Frank Loewen, all right. He'd been the one who, having gotten wind of the proposed lodge from the usual grapevine sources, had come down from Foster Rapids, introduced himself and benevolently offered to lend them money to build when the banks had refused, saying everyone in the community had an obligation to help revive the North. Very soon, since they were now no longer able to keep up their loan payments, Frank would be in a legal position to foreclose and securing an investor would only hasten the process.

"And?" Dane had been staring at her.

"And what?" she returned as she uncrossed her legs and jumped down from the stool. She reached for his empty plate. "What do I know about business?"

Dane grinned up at her. "A lot more than you let on, I think."

"Maybe." She shrugged and dropped the dishes into the sink with a clatter. She needed time to think.

How long had Frank Loewen been running around looking for an investor? And just who had filed the environmental complaint with the government? The whole community had been excited about the project, and everyone who'd had a dime to spare had bought a small share, except the Bird Creek First Nation Band Council, who supported the lodge in theory but had the same reservations towards investing as the banks had. However, they had been willing to let Gilbert recruit several youths from the band to act as guides and hands, and many others would have been employed as drivers, cooks and cleaners etc. They had prime fishing spots selected, a variety of hunting packages developed for each season, birdwatching and wilderness tours planned, and guests could also participate in regular summer and winter sports activities. They had even designed some survival courses. On top of all that, it was hoped the expected economic spinoffs would boost the all-but-dead local economy.

That snake! Frank never missed an opportunity when he was in town to blather on about what an idiotic idea the lodge had been in the first place, and what a fool he'd been to lend them money. The worst part was they were starting to believe it themselves!

"It's obvious you've got something to say about Frank Loewen, why not just tell me? I've found local opinion is usually pretty accurate."

Eve screwed in the sink plug and turned on the taps. "Does it influence your decision about investing?"

"Sometimes."

She poured dish soap into the water and wondered if Frank intended to use the existing plans for the lodge, or if he had ideas of his own. How much did

Dane know about the lodge at Lake of the Wolves, and was he aware that the title for the property was still in her name? Should she tell him? It was obvious he had no idea that Lake of the Wolves was only a day's hike into the bush, not two-hundred kilometres up the road at Foster Rapids. She could only guess Frank was hoping to keep his plans secret by having Dane meet him in Foster Rapids. Just north of Jake's Corner, a temporary service road had been hacked through the bush so that building materials could be hauled in. Frank likely intended to use it, avoiding Jake's Corner altogether. "I'm sure you're an astute businessman," she said at last. "If there is anything about this lodge that isn't what it appears to be, you'll catch it."

Dane didn't reply to her statement. Instead he came over to the sink and grabbed the dish towel hanging above her. "You don't have a dishwasher?"

"Nope. I'm only busy Sunday mornings and sometimes Saturday nights."

His proximity unsettled her. His nearness was far too inviting, and the fact that the future of Jake's Corner could very well rest in his hands in no way diminished her desire to drink in the lingering scent of him.

She turned off the taps, suddenly feeling an overwhelming need to be rid of him. She crossed over to the pickup window and with two fingers in her mouth whistled loudly. "If anyone's going to Foster Rapids today, would you be kind enough to take this man with you?"

A chorus of *no's* and excuses sounded back at her.

She turned back to Dane, shrugging her shoulders in defeat. "Looks like you're here for the day."

FOUR

Dane, to his surprise, didn't at all mind being stranded at the *Last Chance Gas and Grill*. And he had to admit he was glad the phones weren't working. He couldn't remember the last time his despotic Day-Timer hadn't dictated his day.

He wondered mildly if anyone would even notice his absence. Frank Loewen probably thought he had changed his mind or been delayed for some reason. One day wasn't going to make much difference.

It was the minx in the high heels and miniskirt, wiping down tables, who seemed upset at his predicament. She attacked the tables with a vengeance, scouring them until Dane was sure she'd wear off the arborite finish, all the while muttering and mumbling under her breath. He could hear bits of *scumbag* and *snake* and an occasional *Jake* as she scraped the chairs across the floor and slammed them into place under the tables.

Dane opted to stay in the kitchen and clean up the counters. She hadn't asked him to help, but he suspected she'd have been insulted if he offered money for his room and breakfast. Besides, it was safer in the kitchen. If there was one thing he knew about women, it was to steer clear when they were mad and never ask, *What's wrong?*

Her temper had flared up after the breakfast patrons left, particularly Jake. She had asked him outright to drive Dane to Foster Rapids, but Jake had refused with a glare towards Dane, saying in his usual gruff manner that *Sweet-Pea* wasn't running very good since he had to take her out last night without a proper tune-up.

After Jake had left, Eve had cleared the dishes from the tables like a hurricane. Dane kept expecting to hear the music of shattering glass but was surprised the dishes managed to survive her tantrum intact.

She sure was cute! Even in a temper. All that passion ... passion and Eve in the same sentence initiated a wander down what was rapidly becoming a familiar path. He wondered why this sudden attraction to a woman who seemed to be the antithesis of his tastes. He liked them sleek and sophisticated.

Eve was woman untamed and it spilled from all her curves. And yet those dark delicate brows and heavily lashed eyes, gently sloped cheeks and curl of ripe lips hinted at a softness beneath, almost deceiving a man into thinking she would come without a price. She'd be a ride on the wild side, all right, but he'd be afraid to take her anywhere for fear of what she might say or do, and from the little he knew of her, she wasn't the type to let anyone restrain her. In fact, she'd probably do the exact opposite of whatever was expected, just to be contrary. And he was sure she'd have no qualms about telling a person exactly what was on her mind.

He grinned. He would have to keep her under lock and key.

* * *

Eve wasn't sure who to be more mad at: Frank Loewen for stealing her lodge, Jake and his cohorts for leaving her stranded with Dane, or with Dane himself. And as for Dane, she couldn't decide which made her angrier: the fact that he, too, was stealing her lodge or that she liked him despite it.

She'd seen plenty of men just like him through Bryce's business dealings. Men of his ilk were always married to their careers. Appearances counted for everything, and if they were anything like Bryce, they weren't especially monogamous, either. Charmers, yes. Trustworthy? Hardly.

And yet, something about Dane seemed to fit her like skin.

Eve sighed with resignation as she removed the broom from its hook by the cold-room door and began sweeping the floor. Well, she was stuck with him for the day so she might as well make the best of it. She wondered again if she should tell him who really owned the land at Lake of the Wolves. It seemed as if an opportunity to save the lodge had dropped into her lap, and she would be a fool not to give it a try.

A curious, wicked thought crossed her mind as she hung the broom back on its hook. What if Jake already knew why Dane was going to Foster Rapids? What if Stanley and Gilbert also knew?

She slid a glance towards Dane who, with his back to her, was placing a stack of dirty plates into the sink. What if everyone at Jake's Corner knew? It would explain much.

Could it be that Dane's departure from Jake's Corner had been purposely delayed by Jake in order to give her time to somehow convince him to invest in their company instead of buying in with Frank Loewen?

She pulled the large green plastic bag from the kitchen trash can and tied it shut with a silent giggle. If so, then Dane had pretty much been kidnapped. She snuck a glance at Dane again. Jake wouldn't do such a thing, would he?

If her suspicions were correct, and even if they weren't, she reasoned as she ran out the back door and across the grass to the trash bin, she didn't see why she shouldn't take advantage of the opportunity in front of her. Shivering from the fresh nip of autumn air against her bare arms and stocking-clad legs, she unlocked the lid and dropped the bag inside, and despite the desire to hurry back inside to warmth, stood thinking. She'd have to figure out the best way to pitch Dane and wait for a ripe moment. She couldn't just blurt it all out. She carefully relocked the bin against the intrusion of bears and other scavengers, and hugged her arms to herself, shivering as she pondered the back door and what she might say.

The more she imagined how she might broach the subject with Dane, the more ridiculous it sounded even to herself. She and her partners had nothing to offer but desperation and deep debt over an undeveloped piece of land, which, in addition to being mortgaged to the hilt, wasn't worth much in an out-of-reach place like Jake's Corner. Frank, on the other hand, owning the local Foster Rapids watering-hole, would not only appear to be competent and credible but, after repossessing both the land and lodge, would be able to offer Dane an attractive deal.

On top of all that, as likeable as Dane seemed, companies like his didn't get rich by being nice. Nor did they care about what happened to communities like Jake's Corner. On the contrary. If Eve and her partners' predicament were unearthed, Dane might waste no time plundering the remains — he could pay off their loan, scoop up their property and now-nearly-worthless shares and walk away with everything without having to share any of it with Frank. They were in no financial position to stop him and they'd be worse off than before.

The thought was disheartening. It was obviously too risky to tell Dane anything. In fact, they should probably get him out of Jake's Corner and on his way to Foster Rapids before he figured things out himself. She wasn't quite sure how she was going to accomplish that when the whole community seemed so unwilling to help.

He was busily washing dishes and whistling a jolly tune, so involved in his task that he hadn't heard her enter. She grinned at the sight of him up to his elbows in suds and food scraps, his silk shirt sleeves rolled up high over his muscular arms. He must have used a whole bottle of dish soap. A mountain of foam and bubbles billowed over the edges of the sink and was slowly spreading across the counter and dripping down to the floor. Clumps of foam were scattered haphazardly on the wall as if he had tried to beat them down.

He looked so harmless. Perhaps she had him all wrong.

Perhaps she had everything wrong. Jake hadn't kidnapped him. She was just a lonely country gal with a big imagination ready to get her into trouble. Likely, Jake had unplugged the phone for some reason and forgotten to plug it back in, and his *Sweet-Pea* did have a tendency to be temperamental and work when she felt like it rather than when she was needed. As for Stanley and Gilbert, well you never could be too sure of anything with those two. They were an impulsive pair. There could be any number of reasons why they hadn't wanted to help Dane, including — though she seriously doubted it — deciding to honour Sunday as the Lord's Day.

"Really, Dane," Eve's teasing reprimand surprised him, "you're well on your way to creating an environmental disaster with all that soap!"

Dane gave her a wide grin and a display of dimples. "Who'd have thought it was so easy?"

"How much did you use?" she laughed, coming up beside him and grabbing a towel.

He gave her a sheepish, lopsided grin, his green eyes dancing. "I discovered last night in the bath that your water is hard, and since there were a lot of dishes, I dumped in half a bottle and used the sprayer to make it foam. How much do you usually use?"

Eve reached for a plate and began drying it. "Not that much!" she cried. "It's obvious that either you're not a sensitive *millennium man* who does his share of the housework or you've got hired help."

He turned to her with raised brows and a wide, green-eyed, dimpled grin. "Fishing?"

She hadn't consciously been attempting to discern his marital status; she was fairly certain he wasn't married, but since she wouldn't mind knowing for sure ... She gave him a crooked little grin. "No, not necessarily. Married men are typically pretty conspicuous, but since you brought it up ..."

Dane lifted his hands out of the dish water and held them up for her inspection. "See? No ring." He pointed to his right hand and a large school ring sporting a dark blue sapphire. "University hockey championship ..." He dropped his hands back into the water and gave her a wink. "Not even cohabiting."

Eve asked herself if she wouldn't have been happier to learn he was securely attached to someone. At least then she could have designated him as unavailable and extinguished any attraction she felt towards him. The fact that he could be the means of her financial ruin should have been enough to lessen his charm, but it made little difference, and for sure, knowing he was free would only intensify the personal tug-of-war she was already having over liking him but wanting nothing to do with his lifestyle.

"Fair is fair," Dane said with another wink. "Your turn."

He meticulously scrubbed a plate, rinsed it and stacked it in the drying rack. His slow, careful movements spoke of an inherent thoroughness and perfectionism. He would be a man who, once committed to something, saw it through to the end. But then Bryce had been the same way, although he used to pick and choose what he would commit himself to, and his marriage to Eve hadn't been one of them.

"I'm not married," she replied dryly. "Not even close."

"So what is Jake to you?" he asked.

Eve reached for a handful of cutlery and pretended indignation. "Well, he's certainly not my lover! As a matter of fact, after we came to an agreement that I would stay here indefinitely, he moved out to his old family homestead to protect my reputation from gossip."

A loud guffaw erupted from Dane. "You've got to be kidding!"

Eve jammed her hands onto her hips in mock anger. "I think I'm insulted!" she cried, her mouth open peevishly. "Lots of men his age have young wives! Are you saying you don't believe an old man would lust after me?"

Dane rinsed a spatula and grinned over at her. "Ah, Eve ... first you fish for my marital status, now you're fishing for compliments."

"Oh, pleeese!" Eve snorted. "I haven't had to fish for compliments since my braces came off in junior high school."

Dane chuckled. "No, I don't suppose you have. I'll bet you had all the poor young lads running around in circles! I almost feel sorry for them." He plunged a skillet into the soap suds and continued scouring. "So, you still haven't told me how you and Jake fit together."

"He found me, just like he found you."

"You rolled your car, too?"

"No, but I did plow into a snow bank. I'd have frozen to death if Jake hadn't come looking for me."

"How did he know you needed help?"

"I had stopped for gas, same as you, only instead of a thunderstorm, there was a blizzard. Most of the time I could barely make out the front end of my car, let alone see the road ahead. Jake had cautioned me about going on, but in case you haven't noticed," she took the plate he was holding out to her, "I can be stubborn at times, so on I went."

"And a worried Jake came looking for you in that monster he likes to call *Sweet-Pea*?"

Eve laughed softly. "Something like that."

"And?"

"And the rest is history."

He scrubbed the pot she had made the Hollandaise sauce in. "So what brought you out here in the first place? Did you have friends or relatives in the area?"

"I was between jobs at the time." He didn't need to know that she'd been fleeing her shattered marriage, or that she'd been seeking the comfort and advice of her only sibling. "My sister and her husband are wildlife photographers, and they were up in the Foster Rapids area, so I was driving up for a visit. It's rare that we are ever on the same side of the globe, let alone in the same country."

He grinned at her. "Let me guess ... you drove all the way from ... Toronto?"

She grinned back. "Sometimes a long drive is just the thing to clear one's head." Especially if one has nowhere to go, she thought wryly, taking a stack of plates to a cupboard. She couldn't have *gone home to mom*, her father being a widower since Eve's early childhood, and she'd been too ashamed to tell him right away. Besides, he'd been halfway across the world at the time.

She grabbed a new dish towel and picked up the pot he'd finished scrubbing. He stared down at her with a slight frown, as if he suspected her story wasn't as simple as she made it sound. "That still doesn't explain about you and Jake." He smiled slowly. "Or is it unrequited love for Stanley and Gilbert that keeps you here?"

Eve's smile grew. Darn those dimples. Why was it she always fell for the charmers? If she wasn't careful, he'd coax the socks right off her feet.

"Jake brought me back to the *Last Chance* and Mrs. Jake —"

"There was a Mrs. Jake? He actually managed to convince some poor old woman to marry him? What did he do, kidnap her?"

Eve twisted her towel and snapped it at him with a laugh. "He's not always a grouch. Jake can be a warm, loving and generous man ... with a sense of humour, I might add."

Dane let out a loud laugh. "A sense of humour? That's funny in itself." He rinsed a mug and reached for another. "So, if there was a Mrs. Jake, then I assume Jake isn't his first name."

Eve shook her head.

"What is it then?"

"Who knows!"

Dane grinned. "The old crank doesn't use his own name and berates me for taking exception to the misuse of mine?"

"See, I told you he has a sense of humour."

"Okay, you were telling me about you and *The Jakes*. Jake brought —" He broke off, then began again apologetically, "You know, I had just assumed Mrs. Jake was no longer around."

Eve's smile was soft. "She passed away a few years ago. She was a remarkable woman," she added fondly. "When Jake found me, I was frozen almost right through, and Mrs. Jake fed me, gave me a hot bath and tucked me into bed. In the morning, Jake suggested Mrs. Jake could use some help in the kitchen, and the next thing I knew I was passing out meals and washing dishes ... and I've been here ever since."

"Uh — oh, I don't think I like the sound of this," Dane said, his sea-green eyes twinkling down at her. "Am I here forever now, too?"

Eve couldn't hold back another smile. The idea did have a certain appeal. "Well some folks do claim Jake has special powers ... could be you're under his spell."

Dane let the dish cloth drop into the sink. Green eyes frolicked. Dimples cavorted. Wet hands went around her waist and pulled her close. "I'm under a spell all right, of that I'm sure, but I don't think it's Jake's."

Eve's heart began pounding in her chest, his firm, warm body next to hers an inviting contrast to the clinging dampness at the back of her shirt where his hands were. She'd be finished if she let him kiss her. She'd lose much more than her socks, and her pride and self-control would be the first things to go.

She pressed her hand to his lips with a beguiling smile. "I've always understood that part of a spell was to tempt but never gratify the victim."

His eyes still danced. His grin never wavered. He just let her go, stuck his hands back into the dish water and still looking at her, said, "Ah, but are you sure it's me who is the victim and not you?"

Eve thought about Jake and Stanley and Gilbert, the lodge and her earlier suspicions. She grinned back at him. "If anyone's a victim around here, Dane, I'm sure it's you."

FIVE

After they finished cleaning up the kitchen, she suggested a walk. Dane was sorry to see the miniskirt replaced by jeans and a flannel shirt beneath a light, unzipped jacket, but even those couldn't bridle her vibrant sensuality. Being as the contents of his luggage remained strewn about the upside down wreckage of his rented vehicle, his own attire, particulary his shoes, didn't lend well to a trek through the countryside, but Eve had promised to keep to the beaten path and not hike too far.

She took him out the back door, where the only adornments in the small clearing which passed for a yard consisted of an ancient wooden gazebo with peeling paint and torn screens, an old wooden porch swing in an equal state of neglect, and a nearly collapsed outhouse which she assured could still be used in an emergency. Protruding slightly above the dense bush and about a kilometre away, a warped and balding roof could be seen.

"Jake's work-shed," she said.

Following her down a narrow path to the creek, he thought about how he'd almost kissed her in the kitchen. *I'm under a spell* ... geez! He couldn't believe he'd used such a schmaltzy line. Usually, sparkling wit and a dimpled grin were all it took to have a woman lapping from his hand.

His dimpled grins worked on Eve. He could see it.

He had felt it when she was in his arms. There was an undercurrent running between them that he had sensed the moment she had opened the door of the *Last Chance* to sell him gas. An undercurrent that, to him, felt more like a threat than a promise. Eve must have sensed it, too, because she had stopped him from kissing her, though he could tell it was the last thing she wanted to do.

"That's Stanley and Gilbert's garage," Eve announced, pulling him out of his reverie.

Dane looked up to see her pointing in the direction of a battered and weather-beaten structure which, by the angles of its roof, suggested it might have been a barn at one time. The surrounding grounds were cluttered with an archaic tow truck, burned-out cars, back halves of rusted pickup trucks, wheels and rims, and an endless assortment of pieces and parts, all rusted or rusting and all looking more like garbage than inventory. *Gilbert and Stanley's Auto Parts and Repairs* painted boldly on the planking above the well-seasoned double doors completed the picture.

Uncertain as to whether she expected a comment, Dane withheld an opinion and instead asked how long they had been in business.

"Ever since they finished high school," Eve replied, as she led him away from the creek and onto a narrow dirt road. "Stanley had wanted to go to university, but when his mother's health started to fail, he opted to stay here and help take care of her and the kids. Their house is behind the garage and through the trees."

"Where's his father?"

"Ran off when Stanley was ten years old. According to him, he was such a miserable drunk, they were more than happy to see him go anyway."

"And Gilbert?"

"Gilbert never wanted to leave his family, either, so going into business with Stanley was the best solution for them both since they're such good friends. Theirs is the only auto parts or repair garage between Foster Rapids and Thompson, a two-hour drive either way. They manage to do enough business to keep them afloat."

"Hey, Dan, my man!"

Dane raised his head to the sound and laughed inwardly when he realized he was already responding to his new name.

Gilbert had opened a small door at the side of the garage as they approached. Stanley poked his head out behind him. "We was just gettin' ready to go take a look at your truck and see what we'll need to bring out tomorrow."

Dane studied both young men who stood gaping before him with wide, toothy grins that bordered on smirks. They wore identical black leather jackets over crumpled T-shirts and tattered, grease-smeared jeans, and each had pulled his long hair — one head shining black, the other flaming red — into a tight pony tail, which did nothing for either one of them, except emphasize, in Stanley's case at least, a possibly receding hairline.

Dane bet that both their heads together wouldn't equal one brain, but as they were the only thing even remotely resembling mechanics in the area, he supposed that unless he found a phone he might have no alternative but to use their services.

"Thanks, guys, I sure would appreciate that, but I thought you boys didn't work on Sundays," he said amiably, giving them a generous smile.

Stanley stepped out beside Gilbert. "Lookin' ain't workin', Dan," he said, his voice hinting that he thought Dane was a simpleton for needing clarification of something so plain.

"If you're going to bother travelling the distance, why don't you save yourself a trip and winch it up while you're there?" Dane suggested. "It wouldn't be working as much as it would be helping."

Stanley and Gilbert turned to face one another and appeared to think about this for a minute. Stanley scratched his head. Gilbert rubbed his chin.

Finally Gilbert spoke. "Nah, I think that'd be workin'. Just having a look ... well, that'd probably be helpin'." He paused and stretched his lips across his teeth in what Dane assumed was supposed to be a smile. "But since you're worried about us having to make two trips, we'll charge for both, and then you won't have to feel bad."

They were regular little thieves! Dane still suspected that Stanley might not have all of his oars in the water, but he was fairly sure Gilbert merely pretended at stupidity. His insurance coverage would pick up the tab for any expenses involving the vehicle, but their trickery annoyed Dane all the same. His business practices might be shrewd, but he had never cheated anyone and immensely disliked dealing with those who did, although it was often unavoidable.

"Sure, that's fine with me," he said grimly, trying to mask his irritation. "But do you mind if I use your phone before you go?"

Stanley and Gilbert looked at one another in a repeat performance of their earlier charade. Again it was Gilbert who spoke. "Well, now that's a funny thing ... the phone ... it doesn't seem to be working. Is yours working, Eve?"

Dane could have sworn Gilbert's question had caught her off guard. Her eyes darted towards Dane briefly and then swung back to Gilbert. "Uh ... no," she mumbled, then answered more firmly, "No, it's been out all day. I just can't think what could be wrong with it. We'll have to call the phone company and find out what's wrong." Then she giggled at Dane from behind her brown eyes and shrugged her shoulders. "Silly me! How can we *phone* the *phone* company if our *phones* aren't working?"

Dane frowned down at her. "Does this happen often?"

"Never happened before!" "Yes, all the time!" "Sometimes." Stanley, Gilbert and Eve said in unison, their voices overriding one another. All three of them, realizing what they had done, turned first to each other, then back to Dane before swiftly repeating themselves, except each of them said the exact opposite of what they had said the first time.

The furrow of Dane's frown deepened.

Eve returned it with a pretty smile, the kind of pretty smile that makes a big promise it seldom delivers. Vanessa had used it when she was trying to convince him to attend some dull social event with her empty-headed friends.

"You see, Dane," Eve said sweetly, her eyes wells of guilelessness, "it's never happened before that *both* of our telephones aren't working at the same time, and although their phone often doesn't work, mine usually does."

Dane bit back a grin. Evidently, some sort of oddball conspiracy was developing in the minds of these bizarre folks at Jake's Corner. He couldn't imagine what it would be, apart from squeezing a few extra bucks out of the wallet of a poor stranded sap like himself. Maybe Stanley and Gilbert's phone was working, and maybe it wasn't, but short of forcing his way past them to check it out, he was stuck at Jake's Corner until tomorrow morning.

His eyes ran the length of Eve's exquisite form. While she would never win any prizes for her acting ability, that little smile of hers promised far more than Vanessa's ever had. It was almost worth pretending he'd fallen for it.

He set his grin free. So what if it cost him a few extra dollars? He was having fun. Why not go along with the little game the three of them were playing? Who knew where things might end up, particularly where Eve was concerned? This unscheduled delay in his itinerary might prove to be worth the wait.

"I don't understand how you can be so indifferent over your telephones not working," he said gravely. He was a better actor than all three of them put together. "If that happened in Toronto as often as you say it does here, there would be rioting in the streets."

Gilbert nodded his head soberly and Stanley did likewise.

"Of course! And with good reason," Eve said with a wave of her hand and a dulcet voice. "Toronto has the country's economy to run, but here in Jake's Corner, there's never anything so important happening that it can't wait a bit."

Stanley and Gilbert agreed and then tugging black leather baseball caps onto their heads, sauntered off towards their rusted old tow truck. "If you don't mind, Dan, we'll stop by the *Last Chance* later today to let you know how everything's looking with your truck," Gilbert called out from behind the driver's seat as the engine fired up with a mighty roar, hesitated a few times and then settled down to a stumbling idle, the muffler protesting its neglected condition.

Dane gave his head a doubting shake as he

watched the tow truck disappear around the corner, then turned his grin to Eve. "Are you sure they know what they're doing?"

* * *

The only thing Eve was sure about at this moment was that she had not been imagining things. Obviously, everyone in Jake's Corner had learned the purpose of Dane's trip, and there definitely was a plot in motion to keep him from heading on to Foster Rapids. What she truly didn't understand was how they could fool themselves into thinking they could come up with the money to keep Frank from foreclosing. They were out of options. Period. Even the whole town together couldn't scrape up enough funds. And no one had anything of value anymore to put up for collateral. Even their houses were almost worthless; the bank had so much as said so when it had turned down their pledged homes and businesses as security. What value is a house that no one would ever want to live in? Who would ever want to live in a place like Jake's Corner except the hicks who were already there?

Remembering Dane's question, Eve glanced up at him. He was staring at her, puzzlement on his face. The last thing she wanted to do was arouse his suspicion that there was anything out of the ordinary going on at Jake's Corner. She pasted an encouraging smile on her face and grabbing his arm, pulled him along the road. "Don't worry, *Dan*. They're more capable than they appear!"

She had scarcely uttered the words when Stanley and Gilbert's tow truck came screeching back to the garage in a flurry of dust and exhaust fumes.

"Someone's stealin' yer truck!" Stanley hollered,

jumping out while the truck was still in motion, his feet skidding over the gravel. He grabbed a bewildered Dane and pushed him towards the tow truck.

"Where's the local RCMP detachment?" Dane called back to Eve in exasperation, as Gilbert leaned across the cab, grasped him by the shirt collar and tugged him inside, Stanley assisting with a solid shove.

"Well, okay, it hasn't exactly been stolen yet," Gilbert could be heard explaining as Stanley slammed the door with a loud bang of rusted metal.

"I don't believe this!" Dane could be heard groaning from inside.

"Yeah, but Gilbert remembers reading one time," Stanley yelled emphatically over the roar of the muffler, "about how there's a truck stolen in Canada every day, and yours has been there for ... uh ... for at least that long now!"

"Good grief!" Eve heard Dane complain as they sped off and then screeched to a halt.

Gilbert poked his dark head out his window and bellowed out to Eve before squealing off again, "Eve, get rid of the frankfurters! You're makin' people sick."

SIX

"*Frankfurters?*" Eve muttered to herself as she stared after them and watched their trail of dust settle back down onto the road.

She didn't even want to know. What she did want was to try and talk some sense into her partners. Even if by some miracle they had come up with a way to raise money, they were going to blow everything by making themselves out to be complete and utter idiots! Dane was no fool and would not take kindly to being made into one. The zanier their desperate plot became, the more likely he was to uncover it, at which point he might become angry enough to do the very thing they all feared he and his company were capable of: plundering their dreams and leaving them all penniless!

She whirled around and stalked down the road, past Stanley and Gilbert's garage, determined to find Jake. She cut through a crude path in the bush and moments later emerged into a clearing of overgrown grass and weeds where Jake's house sat. His garage door was wide open, but *Sweet-Pea* wasn't in her usual resting place.

She sighed in frustration and headed back the way

she had come. She had just reached Stanley and Gilbert's garage again when the familiar and unwelcome voice of Frank Loewen shouted at her from their parking lot.

"A fellow could rob your place blind! I finally decided to come looking for you."

Eve watched as he swaggered closer, his beer belly proudly preceding him, the wind taking exception to the nest-like hairpiece perched atop his head in a dark mass of gnarled curls. She supposed she couldn't blame Stanley and Gilbert for abducting Dane. They must have passed Frank on their way out to Dane's truck and panicked. Either that or they'd seen his car at the *Gas and Grill*.

"I've never understood why you and Jake just leave the place unattended whenever you have a mind to." He stopped in front of her, his hands on his hips.

"Frank, what an unpleasant surprise," Eve returned with a crisp smile, repulsed by the greedy manner in which he assessed her form. Getting rid of this *frankfurter* would be a pleasure, and unlike Dane, he was easy prey. She marched past him. "Could you come back, in say, fifty years or so? I have some things to attend to."

"Now, Eve," he panted heavily in an effort to keep up, his squat body waddling behind her, "I've come with the purest of intentions ... just looking out for my fellow man."

"Frank, we're all aware of how well you look out for your fellow man," Eve said as she opened the back door and stepped inside the *Gas & Grill* kitchen, not bothering to catch the door as it swung back towards him. "Who's the poor sucker this time?"

Frank caught the door, puffing as he lifted his

pudgy body over the threshold and followed her into the restaurant. "I don't know, but someone's truck is standing on its head about ten kilometres back. I figured maybe you had a Da —" He stopped short and began again slowly, choosing his words carefully. "I wondered if maybe you had a ... uh ... stranded guest who might need reliable transportation to ... to somewhere, seeing as how his — or her — truck is out of commission."

"I didn't see no truck," Jake reported emphatically from the store entrance. He strolled in, placed his cap on the counter and poured himself a coffee. "And I just come that way."

Frank snorted at him. "It's lying there on its back like a turtle with its legs in the air! How could you have missed it?"

"Can't miss somethin' that ain't there," Jake replied tersely and gulped some coffee. "Maybe you should get them eyes checked. Yer seein' things."

"I am not seeing things," Frank snarled, giving Jake a roll of his eyes.

"Ya just said ya seen a truck," Jake exclaimed. "Ain't a truck a thing?" Eve bit her tongue to keep from laughing, thankful Jake had relieved her of the responsibility of sidetracking Frank.

"You're the one who didn't see it," Frank scoffed, "but you're so ancient I'm surprised you can see at all."

"I only see what I see, Frank, not what you see also," Jake replied, unperturbed. He turned to Eve. "What do you see?"

Eve tried to look serious. "Do you mean, like, right now?" She looked around blankly, then affected deep concentration. "Okay, well, I see you and Frank ... should I be seeing a truck as well?"

"You guys can't fool me!" Frank sputtered,

jumping up, nearly knocking his chair over. "You're hiding him, aren't you?"

"The truck's a him?" Eve cried. "How would you know a thing like that?"

"No, the guy in the truck!"

"There's a guy in the truck, upside down?" Eve asked, biting down hard on her lip to keep from laughing. Jake was snickering into his coffee behind Frank's back. "For heaven's sake, why didn't you help him?"

Frank's reddened face ballooned. "Do I have to explain everything to you people?" He clenched his teeth and spouted while Eve watched Stanley and Gilbert's truck whip past the window with Dane's truck in tow, "Don't you think if there was a truck upside down, there'd be a driver?"

"How can anybody drive a truck upside down?" Jake scowled.

"Wait! I do ... I did ... I did see a truck!" Eve exclaimed with glee and pointed behind Frank.

"Was there a guy driving it?" Jake asked.

"How would I know? It wasn't upside down!"

"I've had enough!" Frank blustered, shoving his chair out of the way. "I'm calling the RCMP!"

"Frank, I'd think twice about calling the RCMP and making them drive fifty kilometres to look for a truck being driven upside down," Eve warned. "Besides, the phones are out." She continued a little more empathetically, "But why don't you and Jake go see if you can find this truck, seeing as how you're so upset about it."

"I'm not upset!" Frank bellowed.

"Phew-ee," Jake was shaking his head as he rose and drained the last of his coffee. "Driving a truck upside down. This I gotta see."

"No one's driving a truck!" Frank blurted angrily,

following Jake to the door.

"Yer story keeps changin'," Jake muttered, tugging his cap into place and jangling the keys to *Sweet-Pea* between his gnarled fingers as he stepped outside.

Through the window, Eve watched Frank protest all the way to *Sweet-Pea*, waving his arms dismissively to whatever Jake was saying, pointing angrily towards the highway and at one point appearing to refuse to get into *Sweet-Pea*. She giggled when Frank kicked *Sweet-Pea* behind Jake's back.

She had to admit, despite having been thrown into this idiotic conspiracy, getting Frank all riled up was extremely satisfying. He made it so easy, proud man that he was. Of course, they hadn't fooled him for a moment, but that hadn't been their intention; they had merely wanted to get him out of the way temporarily.

He'd be fuming shortly and racking his brains to figure out how they'd managed to confiscate the truck. He could accuse and threaten all he wanted; it didn't matter. What more could he do to them? He was already practically stealing their land from under their feet.

Dane on the other hand ... it mattered a great deal what Dane thought, since he pretty much held all the cards. She could only imagine what inanity he was having to endure with Stanley and Gilbert. No doubt they'd be detaining him until they were confident Frank was out of the way.

She had to talk to Stanley and Gilbert alone. There had to be a more sane way of going about this, a way that wouldn't backfire or arouse Dane's anger. She glanced at the phone and wondered if the repair shop's was actually unplugged. Did she dare call?

What if Dane heard it ring, or worse, answered it?

She paced a moment, biting on her lower lip, trying to decide what her next move should be. "Oh for Pete's sake," she griped as she slipped back into her running shoes and ran out the back door.

* * *

Dane watched Stanley and Gilbert lower his rented truck to the ground and shook his head with a grin which he hid behind a pretense of studying his dust-covered shoes. It had been the ride of a lifetime, he'd give them that much. He'd been surprised their tow truck had been able to maintain a steady, full-out speed of one-hundred-twenty kilometres per hour without falling apart, although at one point the hood did fly open in blatant protest before immediately slamming shut again when they bounced hard into yet another pothole.

It had been while they were winching up his truck that he realized they were hardly the inept jokers they pretended to be. Only skilled tradesmen could have accomplished what they had with such lightning speed and accuracy. He'd scarcely had time to climb out of the cab when his vehicle swiftly rose off its back and onto its wheels without any additional scratches. He'd easily agreed with them that he shouldn't drive it before they looked it over, but he hadn't seen the need to race back to Jake's Corner at breakneck speed. Not that there'd been any sane reason to race out to get the truck in the first place. He'd looked back at the truck, its wheels barely touching the road as they raced along, and had been glad he'd only rented it. Although, from the looks of it now, it didn't appear to be any worse for the ride.

Their verbal shenanigans had been relentless both there and back, one cornball account for their actions after another, and the idiocy continued unabated even now as they poked their heads under the hood, scrutinizing the engine, pausing to twist the occasional part with their wrenches.

"I don't know, Gilbert," Stanley said, squinting up at his partner as he bent down to inspect the undercarriage, "maybe we should put her on the hoist."

"I remind you, Stanley, that today is still Sunday for a couple of more hours yet," Gilbert replied soberly, squatting beside him to peer underneath as well.

"Yeah, okay, but we *helped* Dan when we saved his truck from being stolen. You said it was okay to help on Sundays. Is lookin' her over helpin' or workin'?" Stanley asked, squatting even lower than his partner and sticking his head right underneath.

"Are we going to charge Dan for looking it over, Stanley?" Gilbert inquired much like one asks a less intelligent, younger sibling.

"Do you think we should?"

"Isn't it how we make a living? We can't go around just helping folks all the time."

Stanley stood up, placed his hands on his hips and gesticulated at Gilbert. "Well, the way I see it then, Gilbert, we oughta charge Dan for towing his truck here, but then that'd be workin'."

"Well, then, we can't charge him, can we?"

"But hospitals are open on Sundays. Folks work in hospitals on Sundays. They're helpin' but they're workin', too, right?"

"So, maybe we should charge him for the tow," Gilbert declared. "I suppose we can't help it if our help is work as well."

"What do you think, Dan?" Stanley asked. Both men turned to him, their faces blandly quizzical.

Dane observed them in amused silence before answering. On the way back from retrieving his vehicle, the discussion had centred around which of them had forgotten to tie down the crank-throttle and whose fault it would be if it worked its way loose and whether or not Dane would have to pay to have it fixed, seeing as it would likely be their fault, not his, and on their banter had gone.

Dane had never had much luck working on engines himself, but he was fairly certain there was no such thing as a crank-throttle, but he hadn't seen the need to tell them so, as they seemed to be enjoying their game so much. Watching them had been entertainment in itself. Why they persisted in their charade of stupidity he might never know, but at least now he had a working vehicle again. If worse came to worse, and in the event his keys inadvertently disappeared, as he strongly suspected they might, he could always hot-wire the truck if he found he needed to escape Jake's Corner

He still hadn't been able to piece together the motive behind Stanley and Gilbert's obvious efforts to stall his departure, but his innate sense of character told him, while they were definitely determined, they weren't malicious fellows.

"From a business perspective," he said, after a long pause and with an inward grin, "Gilbert is right. Your work involves helping, so you might say that choosing to work on Sunday is a form of helping, but it's also your work, therefore, you should charge me. However, I didn't ask you to help after you said you couldn't. So was your help, then, not charity? Do you charge for charity?"

The grin couldn't be contained as he watched Gilbert and Stanley blink at him, trying to digest his intentionally tangled response. He could have exploded into a tirade several hours ago and insisted upon having his truck repaired or demand they stop playing him for a fool, but he had to admit, he was enjoying himself, and his curiosity was aroused. He'd always liked a good game of chess, and he usually won. What these local yokels had up their sleeves would be amusing to uncover, but what was more, if he was honest with himself, he welcomed the diversion. He'd been working almost non-stop lately, ever since he'd called it quits with Vanessa, and this was better than any vacation he could have dreamed up.

"Hmm ..." Stanley mumbled finally, his fingers thoughtfully cupping his chin. "It's a real dilemma, isn't it Gilbert?"

"Maybe you should run it by your Minister," Dane suggested, his grin still wide.

"Now, there's an idea," Stanley replied and then added somberly, "except he won't be back until next Sunday comes around. Do you think you could wait that long?"

"Hey! I know!" Gilbert exclaimed, as if the thought had suddenly occurred to him. "I'll go ask Eve. And look, what luck! Here she comes!"

Dane's eyes followed the direction Gilbert pointed in, and he knew the real reason he wasn't in any hurry to leave Jake's Corner. She strode along the path with determined purpose, the savage wind whipping her chestnut hair wildly across her face. The supple movement of her lithe body made his head swim as he watched the gentle swell of her chest rise and fall beneath her shirt, her hips swaying with her stride.

Gilbert trotted out to greet her, the young native's own hair blowing about darkly behind him despite its ponytail. As he neared Eve and slowed his pace, it occurred to Dane that these two people had once been lovers. It was in the way they approached each other, as if each knew the other's thoughts, and the gentle, near imperceptible, way each touched the other's arm. He envied Gilbert for having had what he had never known. What would it be like to have a woman such as Eve love you? To have those dark eyes rest upon you, the fire for you growing in them? To have those vibrant lips open to your kiss? To lose yourself inside her very soul?

"She does that to all of us."

Stanley's crisp voice, devoid of its customary dullard manner, intruded on his thoughts. Dane glanced over at him. He had been watching Dane watch Eve and Gilbert.

Stanley lowered himself onto a dolly and laying flat, slid underneath Dane's truck. "Gilbert was the only one who came close, but even he doesn't have what it takes. Good luck, cause you'll need it," he said huskily before he started banging on something with a hammer, the clang of metal hitting metal ringing throughout the shop.

Dane stared down at Stanley's booted feet protruding from under the truck and asked himself if he had imagined Stanley's brief interlude of sanity amidst the chaos of the day. He grinned. He'd been dropped smack in the middle of the kookiest one-horse town on the planet.

He permitted his eyes to wander out the window to where Eve and Gilbert were now having an animated discussion in the afternoon sun. He might as well interrupt whatever new scheme they were cooking up together for he was fairly certain Eve was embroiled in the intrigue as well, although she seemed less enthusiastic than her pals. He suspected luring her into divulging the local secret would be no small task, but it would be a helluva lot of fun trying.

* * *

"Eve," Gilbert reasoned, "there is no other way! We don't have time to sit around and hash out some elaborate and believable plot to keep Newson around. We just have to wing it. He already thinks we're complete morons, so why disappoint him? As long as he thinks we're nothing but inept losers, it'll never even cross his mind that we have a stake in the lodge." He paused and grasped her by the shoulders. "Besides, what choice do we have? And so what if he uncovers our plot? We're going to lose everything to either Loewen or Newson. If we can buy a few days' time, that'll give the Band Council time to reconsider investing, and they are reconsidering because I approached them about it last night."

"They weren't interested anymore than the banks were. What's changed?"

"Think about it, Eve. A guy like Newson arrives in town, looking to spend money. And he's got plenty of it. My third cousin in Toronto says they're big. He knew the name right away. He hears they're cutthroats. They want — they get. If our little lodge has garnered their interest, it's gotta be worth something, maybe more than we realized. On top of all that, the Band Council fears an outside company may not hire locals. I've told them they wouldn't have to contribute all that much. We only need enough to keep up our loan payments and buy some supplies to finish the lodge. We practically built it ourselves anyway. Surely we can finish it. Once we're up and running, we're home free."

Eve was beginning to waver and knew Gilbert could see it. She dug at the dirt with the toe of her shoe. Maybe he was right. And it had been *her* crazy idea to build a lodge in the first place. She had been the one who convinced everyone to invest and, more important, accept Frank's loan. Didn't she owe them at least an attempt to save their livelihoods?

"What do you owe this guy anyways?" Gilbert asked and grinned. "Besides, you couldn't really classify what we're doing as criminal. He's free to leave anytime he wants ... he just has to walk, is all. I can't help it if his truck isn't running and the phones are out."

Eve expelled a heavy sigh. Gilbert placed an arm on her shoulder. She didn't owe Dane Newson anything. But Gilbert ... long ago they had realized that their affection for each other didn't work as lovers, but he was still her best friend. She just wasn't sure she could handle Dane. A couple of hours was one thing ... but a few days? He had a way of making her forget all she'd learned about men. She'd barely escaped their near kiss in the kitchen. The worst part about it was that she wished she hadn't.

"I know it's a long shot," Gilbert pleaded.

Eve chewed on her lip, knowing she'd already lost the argument. Gilbert knew it, too. She'd just have to take her chances with Dane. She looked past Gilbert as Dane emerged from the garage and headed their way. She couldn't suppress a smile. Maybe she was making too much of it. What harm was there in a little flirting when he made it so much fun? A kiss or two with him, if it came to that, wouldn't kill her, would it? He'd be gone in a couple of days anyway. "What about Frank?" She lowered her voice. "He's already snooping around."

Picking up her cue, Gilbert also lowered his voice. "Loewen is barely an issue. It's not difficult to send him packing."

She gnawed on a knuckle. Dane was only steps away. "I don't know ... I hate lying."

"No one's asking you to," Gilbert grinned, whispering. "We'll do the deceiving, you just be yourself and keep Newson entertained. His tongue's already hanging out so far we're all tripping over it."

She gave him a crooked grin. "You're lucky he's good looking. You'd have never stiffed me with Frank."

"Give us a couple of hours," Gilbert chuckled under his breath as he sauntered off towards the garage.

Dane came up behind the retreating Gilbert, a boyish grin on his face. "As I don't appear to be going anywhere, any time soon, do you think it's possible to finish our walk before I'm shanghaied again?"

"What makes you so sure you're safe with me?" Eve asked with a laugh, knowing he had no idea it was her job to waylay him a little longer.

He leaned close to her, and Eve knew from the glint in his eye and the pounding in her chest that she had her work cut out for her. "Oh, I'm certain I'm not safe with you. The question is, are you safe with me?"

* * *

He was enjoying watching her composure unravel. She pushed him away with a playful hand to his chest, then led him on a seemingly aimless stroll, leaving Stanley and Gilbert to do heaven-only-knew-what to his truck. Before long, she was chattering away, pointing out places of local interest and citing historical anecdotes, leaving Dane with a sense of being on a conducted tour.

"That ridge along the horizon," she said, pointing in the direction of the setting sun, "is the outer boundary of the Bird Creek First Nation where Gilbert lives when he's not sleeping in the auto shop. It's named for Bird Creek, which runs through it and behind Jake's Corner all the way to Lac du Pecher."

"So, I take it the creek you're speaking of is the same one we crossed awhile back?" Dane asked, watching her full lips move as they formed her words, not the least bit interested in what she was saying. Would those lips taste as delicious as they looked?

"Yes," she answered and continued, "You'll notice we're quite a small community at Jake's Corner. There is no school, post office or town hall. Jake supplies folks with a few basic groceries, staples mostly, but everything else we have to get in Thompson. Stanley's mother has a fairly big house and so it doubles as a church and clinic when the pastor or the nurse passes through, either that or we go to Bird Creek First Nation."

A small community was an understatement, Dane

thought as he followed along the path behind her. Impoverished was a more accurate description. The bleak lifestyle at Jake's Corner startled him. Young people were a scarce commodity, and when he looked around, he could see why.

There was nothing to drive the economy. And as far as he could tell, there never had been, other than the reservation. He suspected Jake's Corner had sprouted up around the *Last Chance Gas & Grill*, which had likely garnered a small trade when the mine at Foster Rapids was in operation. The mine, he knew, had closed down a few years ago.

Jake's Corner exuded an air of finality and staleness, which even Eve's brightness couldn't fully diminish. Dane wondered how it was that she seemed so settled here, and why wasn't she married? Somebody should have snapped her up by now. According to Stanley, despite Eve's obvious affection for Gilbert, even he had not been able to possess her.

Now there's a strange word, Dane thought to himself with a self-deprecating grin. Possess. But it did describe what he felt. He didn't want to think in terms of any part of her belonging to anyone else when he thought about even the simple act of kissing her. Did she do that to all men or just him?

"Gilbert's aunt is the local midwife," Eve was saying, and Dane realized he hadn't been listening to her at all.

He decided he didn't care who else she did it to — she did it to him. She was stepping over a log, her head down, still chattering. He caught her hand and tugged her towards him so that she stumbled off balance and fell into his waiting arms. He clamped them around her soft warm body, allowing her no escape. "Eve, shut up and kiss me," he murmured before he finally tasted those lips.

* * *

Had she been waiting for this? All her life.

There had been the ineffectual stolen kisses of an occasional love-struck young boy who took to hanging around the *Last Chance* and helping out. There had been the ardent kisses of the one or two men she had met and briefly dated at Jake's Corner. There had been Bryce's kisses, passionate but selfish to the core.

And then there was Dane's kiss.

It went all the way down to her toes and right back up again. It was passionate, but it gave as much as it took. It emptied and it filled. It was tender, it was fire. It soothed, and it made her ache, and when it was over, she stared up at him in open amazement.

He kissed her again.

This kiss was different. Lethal.

Dane lowered her to the ground, showering her face with tiny kisses, his warmth driving away the cold and the last of her will. Eve began to panic. Had she learned nothing from Bryce? If she didn't get up off the ground now ...

His mouth covered hers again, his fingers tugging at the shirt tucked in at her waist. She turned her head aside and murmured, "We shouldn't." Shivers ran through her as his lips sought her neck, then brushed over her mouth. He kissed her eyes closed. "Dang ... Dan ... Dane ..." she uttered, her mind a fog.

She felt his lips smile against her cheek. When she opened her eyes, he was grinning down at her.

"Really, Eve, I'm hurt. You should at least know my name."

"... but I don't know you," she whispered earnestly.

His grin faded ever so slightly, and his eyes held hers for a moment before wandering off into the dusky distance. When he looked down at her again, there was a softness in their green depths. "I'm sorry. It was only supposed to be a kiss."

SEVEN

To her surprise, Eve found she was blushing as he helped her to her feet.

It wasn't that his kiss had been so intimate or his touch as a lover's. It was that he had, without her consent, made her want to love again. Heaven help her if ever he discovered that. She sighed heavily as she brushed the dirt and autumn leaves from her clothes, then smiled wryly at herself. *A kiss or two wouldn't kill her?*

"I believe you were telling me about the local midwife," Dane said slowly. She could hear his grin.

Eve glanced up at him, knowing his grin was meant to put her at ease and dispel the awkwardness. Her smile grew. Was there no end to his charm? "Yes, well, I think the guided tour is finished for the day," she said lightly, now brushing imaginary dirt from her jeans.

His dimples deepened. "I have to admit, I like how it ended."

She couldn't resist matching the glint in his eye with her own. "Wait 'til you get the bill," she quipped, turning her back to him and heading down the path that led back to the *Gas and Grill*.

* * *

He chuckled quietly as he followed her. She was

something special. Stanley was right; she drove every man in Jake's Corner wild, and he'd just joined their ranks. Something had happened to him when he had kissed her.

It was supposed to have been a simple kiss. He'd had no thought of anything more. Well, okay, he had thought of more, he admitted as he watched her stoop under a low branch, but he had merely intended to feel out the strength of her attraction to him. A kiss was usually enough to let him know where he stood with a woman, but Dane had been the one surprised.

While Eve's response had definitely been much stronger than he had expected, it had been his own reaction that had caught him off guard. The taste of her lips had been shockingly sweet in comparison to how worldly she appeared, an innocence mingled with hesitation, as if she were afraid of herself rather than him. He had kissed her with a gentleness he hadn't known he possessed, and when he kissed her again, it was as if everything in his universe ceased to exist except this mystifying enchantress who wanted to be loved and whom, for that moment, he wanted to love.

He hadn't been watching how closely he followed Eve and a branch she'd pushed past snapped back and stung his face like a whip. He shook his head and laughed at himself. Yep, Stanley was right. He was becoming as noodle-headed as the rest of them.

He followed her out into the clearing across from the *Gas and Grill*. She turned back to give him a shy smile that made him ache to kiss her again. He smiled back. Maybe later.

"Weird things are goin' on around here, I don't care what you say!" a voice bellowing from the front of the building crashed in on his thoughts. A vehicle door slammed loudly. "First the truck vanishes and now my car!" the same voice continued somewhat muffled.

Whose truck could they be talking about? Dane wondered with a grin, certain there could only be one. He quickened his pace and rounded the corner of the *Gas and Grill* just ahead of Eve, in time to witness Stanley frantically shoving, with a booted foot, the large rear-end of a squat man into the cab of the tow truck, Gilbert again ready at the wheel, with the engine running. The truck roared off in a cloud of dust with Stanley, only one foot inside, dangling desperately from the door.

Dane bit back a wide grin. It was almost comforting to see that things at Jake's Corner had reverted to their customary insanity.

* * *

Eve ran up behind Dane in time to see Stanley and Gilbert screech away with Frank Loewen wedged between them in the seat. She'd been so intent on eluding Dane that she'd completely forgotten about Frank. It was sheer luck that Stanley or Gilbert, and not Frank, had discovered her and Dane's approach. They must've seen them from inside the restaurant.

She cast a fast glance towards Dane's face to assess what he'd seen or what he might be thinking, but it was curiously bland, apart from the secretive twinkle in his eyes when he looked back at her.

"I wonder if they've finished with my truck," he mused. "Or are they off on another rescue mission, do you think?"

That secretive twinkle worried her. "It's possible," she replied, grasping at the first explanation to come to mind while trying to mentally devise a means to discover his thoughts, "but they are a flighty pair. You never can tell what they'll do next. One minute they're busy doing something, and the next thing you know they're off doing something else. I guess that's why it takes them so long to finish a job sometimes."

His hands casually in his pants pockets, Dane stared down at his shoes a moment, apparently lost in his thoughts. "I suppose I should be grateful they've assisted me as much as they have," he said, his twinkling green eyes contradicting his somber voice, "after all, it is Sunday."

"Oh yes!" Eve replied agreeably as they mounted the steps of the *Gas and Grill*. "I think they've been quite generous with their time."

"Unfortunately, if they've made no progress, you'll most likely be saddled with me for another night."

From the wide grin he beamed down at her as he held the door open, Eve surmised he wasn't the least bit disappointed about staying another night, a sentiment she was sure was a result of the kiss he'd given her in the bush.

The mere thought of that kiss set her skin on fire. It would take every last ounce of willpower she possessed to resist those dancing eyes and that sandy hair with its flecks of grey and those broad shoulders she just knew would willingly bury her in their embrace with the smallest amount of encouragement from her. What had she gotten herself into by agreeing to Gilbert's hare-brained plan? There was no way he could stay with her another night!

"If it's uncomfortable for you in some way ..." He paused, blocking her way into the restaurant, dimples still grinning down at her. "I could always stay at Jake's ... although I'm not so sure he'll want my company."

For Eve, unable to pull her eyes away from his, the convenience store had suddenly grown quite small, although she suspected that even if he'd been in the other room, he'd have been too close. She realized that he had just challenged her. If she admitted that she would prefer he stay with Jake, she might just as well come out and tell him she'd lost her head to him, and then, of course, like any hot-blooded male, he'd pursue her relentlessly. She knew she didn't have the strength to withstand a full onslaught of seduction no matter how many times she told herself that, beneath the surface, Dane was just another Bryce. She liked him too much and she'd been alone much too long.

She'd just have to stay one step ahead of him all the time. She smiled far more confidently than she felt and hoped he fell for it. "I'm not the least bit concerned about where you stay. Jake's or here ... it makes no difference to me."

He returned her smile. "So it's settled then," he said, his words sounding more like a promise than a statement. "You know, Eve," Dane said lightly, almost conversationally, from behind her as they walked into the restaurant, "maybe I've seen too many movies, but I get the strangest feeling that I've been kidnapped."

Eve's heart jumped into her throat. "Kidnapped?" she croaked, not daring to turn around and face him.

"Yeah, I know it's weird," he laughed, but she could hear a seriousness underneath, "but the way Stanley and Gilbert drove off with that other man just now was reminiscent of how they'd practically dragged me away this afternoon, and I can't help but wonder if there is someone here at Jake's Corner you people don't want me to see."

"That's the silliest thing I've ever heard," Eve bubbled as lightly as she could while she went to the coffee maker and put on a fresh pot. She wouldn't need it; Sunday evenings seldom saw a visitor in the *Gas and Grill*, but it gave her something to do while she kept her back to Dane. "What motive could anyone here have for something like that?"

"I have no idea, Eve. I thought you might be able to tell me."

This time she looked at him, confident in where she could direct the conversation. "Dane, you're welcome to check my deep-freeze, if you like, but the last time I looked, it didn't contain any dismembered body parts." She paused, the empty coffee pot in her hand, and cast him a dark look. "But then again, maybe that's because we're fresh out. Come to think of it, it has been awhile since we've had red meat."

Dane laughed and walked over to her. He grasped her by the elbows. She could feel the heat of his touch through the sleeve of her shirt. "Eve," he said softly, relieving her of the pot and putting his arms around her waist, "if you look into my eyes and tell me everything that is happening here is pure circumstance, I will believe you. If it's not, tell me what you want and maybe I can help you. You don't have to kidnap me."

Would he really help them? Eve asked herself as she stared up at him, knowing from his eyes that he'd see the lie in hers if she told one. Evasion was her only option. She gave him a syrupy smile. "Why would I or anyone else at Jake's Corner want to kidnap you?"

His eyes remained on hers. "I've been at this game for many years, Eve. Just say yes or no. Is my continued stay here happenstance?" He drew her against his hard, muscular body.

Being in his arms again was more dangerous and exhilarating than the first time, since her senses were still reeling from that kiss. If he kissed her now, she was finished. She'd spill the beans on everyone.

"What's a feller got tah do to git somethin' tah eat?" Jake's unexpected presence in the doorway was a godsend.

Dane didn't immediately release her. Instead, he nuzzled her ear and whispered into it, "If I have been kidnapped, Eve, I'm not necessarily complaining." With that, he let her go, nodded a greeting to Jake and climbed the stairs two at a time. Not until she heard his door open and shut did she breathe a sigh of relief.

Jake's wizened face was sheepish. "I suppose maybe I could have come back a little later ..."

Eve crumpled into the nearest chair and put her face in her hands. "You were just in time, Jake. If Dane asks me again, I won't be able to lie," she moaned. "Can't you make Stanley and Gilbert stop?"

Jake scraped a chair across the floor and straddled it, leaning his scrawny arms across the back. "What's he asking you, honey?" he asked, scratching his bristly chin.

"After he saw Stanley and Gilbert drive off with Frank, he asked me who it was we didn't want him to see, not to mention that he's insisting none of the events are circumstantial. And I have to agree that even a fool wouldn't believe the going's on around here. For Pete's sake, twice in one day Stanley and Gilbert shanghai someone into their truck. It's not normal, and Dane knows it."

Jake scraped his chair again as he pushed it back and shuffled over to the coffee pot. "You can handle him. There ain't been a feller you couldn't handle, not that I seen anyways."

It's not him I'm worried about, Eve thought as she watched him pour cream into his mug. *It's me.* "How can I possibly handle him when Stanley and Gilbert are behaving like a pair of lunatics? I'm having to make up excuses for them every five minutes, and half the time I don't have a clue what they're up to myself!"

He shuffled back, turned his chair forward, scraping the floor again, and sat down. He sipped his coffee thoughtfully. "Everything will work out just fine, Eve. Maybe he ain't such a bad feller after all. A bit citified ... but not so bad as you couldn't knock it out of him," he mumbled, not looking up.

Eve jerked her head up. "What on earth are you talking about?"

"It ain't so bad to fall in love again," he muttered between gulps of coffee, his eyes strangely shifty and not daring to meet hers.

"I am not falling in love with Dane Newson!"

"I didn't say you was."

"Well, what, then? Are you insinuating that I *should* fall in love with him?"

"Nope." He drained his cup and shuffled over to her, tugged his cap back on and gave her a weak pat on her shoulders. "I was just wonderin' ... what's the worst that could happen, is all?" he asked slowly before he drifted out the door.

Eve stared after him in open-mouthed horror. *Falling in love ... that was the worst thing that could happen!*

* * *

Dane unplugged his laptop computer from the telephone jack he'd found in the wall behind his bed and then snapped it shut. Obviously, they hadn't rummaged through his luggage or they'd have found the computer in his briefcase, or maybe, he reasoned, they hadn't remembered the phone jack in his room. Normally, he could access his email through his cellular phone, but Stanley and Gilbert wouldn't let him charge it up in his truck, using the excuse they might send a reverse charge through it when they worked on the engine. They had offered, however, to hang onto his cellular phone for him until such time as they could safely recharge it. He'd let them have it, thinking it might be to his advantage for them to believe they had him in a corner.

He slid the bed back into place and dusted himself off. He expected Diane would have an answer for his email, which he'd sent to her home, sometime late tomorrow. If there was anything to be found out about the clowns at Jake's Corner, Diane, his assistant, would track it down. The woman, old enough to be his mother and more ornery than a drill sergeant, was worth her weight in gold, and he paid her accordingly. If he knew her the way he thought he did, she'd already be working her magic on the Internet and be ready to work on the file first thing in the morning.

He looked at his watch and decided to wait before going downstairs to supper. Instead, he pulled the file on the lodge at Lake of the Wolves from his briefcase and reread his notes on Frank Loewen. He was almost embarrassed to realize he hardly knew anything about the man. It was unusual for him to go out on the road so unprepared.

He tossed the file onto the bed and raked a hand through his hair. After calling it quits with Vanessa, he had just wanted to get out of Toronto for a few days. Maybe it had hit him harder than he thought. Maybe she had been right. Maybe it was time he settled down.

He picked up the file again and fanning through it, speculated as to what Eve's stake in keeping him at Jake's Corner could be, then shook his head at the insanity of trying to figure it out. There were a million possibilities but Diane would unearth it for him. Whatever Eve's reason, the way she blew hot and cold over him, she was evidently of two minds about it. He grinned. Playing cat-and-mouse with the folks at Jake's Corner was made all the more fun by her presence. A little more persuasion and she'd tell him everything. She wasn't the hard case she pretended to be. Underneath that sassy exterior was a tender-hearted woman.

He slipped the file back inside his briefcase, unable to lock the broken clasp, a casualty of his accident. He couldn't say that Vanessa had been tender. Brilliant, capable, purposely seductive. Those words described her better. Eve wasn't seductive; she was sensual, but unintentionally so. It was simply her nature.

The sound of several vehicles aroused him from his reverie. He crossed to the window and recognized a few of the people he'd seen earlier at breakfast climbing out of an assortment of trucks and cars. More vehicles were approaching from the highway.

He recalled Eve telling him that the *Gas and Grill* didn't get much business on Sunday evenings, but apparently tonight was to be an exception. He laughed quietly. He might as well go on downstairs and subject himself to the latest scheme about to be foisted upon him. He buried his computer beneath the clothes in his now-battered suitcase, just in case someone came snooping. He stepped into the hallway, grinning widely. He was in no hurry to worm any secrets out of Eve. Trapped in the middle of nowhere with a beautiful and intriguing woman to woo? They could keep him around for as long as they wanted.

* * *

Good grief! Eve thought to herself as half of Jake's Corner pulled up to the *Gas and Grill*, then realized, as still more vehicles came into view, that all of Jake's Corner was pulling up to the *Gas and Grill*.

While she watched, dumbfounded, they loudly filed into the restaurant with *Hey, Eve!'s,* shifting chairs and tables to find themselves places, some of them seeking extra chairs from the stack against the back wall. What on earth had Jake and the boys cooked up now? Jake avoided her eyes when he slipped past her with the others and seated himself at the back of the restaurant.

"Hey there, Dan! Why don't you come sit at our table. We can make room for one more," Andrew Cook called out as he lifted an empty chair off the floor, making Eve aware that Dane was standing directly behind her.

She turned and found herself face to face with his chest. He'd changed into a sweatshirt, but she could still see the outline of the hard muscles beneath. Oh for heaven's sake! Was that the only thing she could think about whenever he came near her? What was he doing standing so darn close anyway? She shook free of the grasp he'd had on her arm, possibly to prevent her from stumbling when she had turned, but as far as she knew she hadn't stumbled.

He was grinning; half of it for her, she was sure, and the other half for Andrew. "Thanks anyway, but I think I'll earn my keep and give Eve a hand in the kitchen."

"Now, Eve, don't work him too hard," Andrew called out as Eve led Dane into the kitchen. "He can't help being stranded out here in the middle of nowhere ... just a string of bad luck. Could happen to anybody."

"Happened to Willard last month ..." Eve could hear someone else affirming as the door swung shut behind her. She shook her head. Subtlety was a lost art in Jake's Corner.

"Should I put on a frilly apron and go take orders?" Dane asked, leaning against the door frame, watching with amusement as she turned on the grill and the fryer.

She couldn't help but laugh a little. "Only if you promise to wear high heels as well."

"Will I look as terrific in them as you did this morning?"

She smiled, warmed by the compliment. "I certainly hope not!"

Andrew Cook stuck his head inside the pickup window, interrupting their banter. "Seems like most folks only want french fries tonight, Eve," he said with a slick grin.

Now there's a big surprise, Eve thought, knowing they were only ordering to justify their presence in the restaurant for Dane's sake. She shuddered at what Dane must be thinking.

"But I couldn't help but notice as how it seems like the whole town is here tonight, too," Andrew continued. "I can't think of anyone who isn't here. I even said so to my wife." He turned to the crowd behind him. "Is there anybody not here?"

They responded with a resounding *Nope!* and a few *Not-so-far-as-I-can-tell's,* although one person called out, "Except for old Hank Brown."

"That's cause he died last winter," someone else called back and everyone laughed again.

Andrew turned back to Eve. "Yep, looks like we're all here. If a person didn't want to be seen, it's just too bad, since we're all here. I can see everyone, and they can all see me." Then he twisted his face towards Dane, craning his neck through the pickup window. "Coincidences like this go on all the time around here."

Dane chuckled. "I'm sure they do, but you've forgotten about Stanley and Gilbert."

"We all try to forget Stanley and Gilbert as much as we can," Andrew snickered and was still snickering at his own joke when he was grabbed from behind and hoisted over the heads of Bob Sanderson and Fred Dyck.

Eve shook her head despairingly. Everyone at Jake's Corner had lost their minds. She was utterly convinced of it as she watched Bob and Fred cart Andrew out the door, insisting that if they didn't leave right now, they might miss the last Canadian goose hunt of the season. Andrew was yelling for them to put him down and that he hated goose hunting.

Eve ran to a window. They shoved Andrew into the front seat of Bob's beat-up old car and drove away, Andrew hollering all the while and banging on the windows.

Dane came up and stood at her elbow. He watched in silence for a moment and then his dancing green eyes met hers. "I suppose this happens all the time, too?"

Eve swallowed hard and looked out the window to avoid his gaze, shrugging her shoulders slightly. "Dane, you've been here one full day. Does it seem out of the ordinary to you?"

He chuckled softly in her ear, causing a shiver to run down her neck. "No. That's the frightening thing. It's starting to feel quite normal."

EIGHT

Yep! It was starting to feel too normal, Dane thought later as he watched her bid farewell to the last of her guests. Life at Jake's Corner was rapidly coming to feel almost comfortable in a wacky way. She locked the front door and then turned to face him.

She stared at him a moment and then said, "Well, that's that."

She walked past him and into the kitchen, which she'd cleaned up earlier, given her patrons hadn't ordered much except coffee. He followed her in and watched her from the doorway, his arms folded across his chest. "So what do you do with the rest of your evenings after everyone leaves?"

She gave him a brief glance like she'd been doing all evening. She'd been afraid to really look at him ever since he'd kissed her. He smiled and waited for her to answer.

"Oh ... usually Stanley or Gilbert picks me up and we work on one of their vehicles," she said, keeping her back to him and rinsing out the coffee pots.

"Every night?" he asked, enjoying her uncharacteristic nervousness, knowing he was the cause.

She shrugged. "Not every night. Sometimes we play street hockey or baseball, or maybe we drive down to Thompson, and I watch them drink beer, and maybe I'll do a little dancing. In the winter we're out on the snowmobiles a lot. If it's unbearably cold, we play cards or watch movies."

"Doesn't anyone ever treat you like a woman and take you out on a date?"

That made her laugh. She turned to him, a wet dish rag in her hands. "Well, I suppose you could call a three-day hike through the bush to go hunting a date, but there seems to be a shortage of hot spots, and since the only fine dining is my own cooking, I'm afraid learning the finer points of car maintenance is as good as it gets."

Dane asked himself who she would be going on three-day hikes with and immediately thought of Gilbert. Had they slept in the same tent or the same sleeping bag? Maybe they hadn't even bothered with sleeping bags. He found himself envying Gilbert once again, this time for bringing Eve into a world he knew little about. What would he do with her in Toronto? Take her to one of the jazz clubs he frequented? A fancy restaurant or two? Dancing?

" ... but I have to say the best was when Stanley taught me how to ride a dirt bike ..."

He'd missed what she'd been saying, and realized that besides work, he had very little else in his life. It had been work, social events with Vanessa and more work. Until tonight, he'd thought he lived a full life. Now it seemed rather dull.

"What do you do, Dane, when you're not working?" she asked, almost as if she'd read his thoughts.

He could feel the sheepishness on his face. "I think I work."

She had such a beautiful smile. "You work so hard for success and all you get with it is more work?"

"I think I thought I was having fun," he said, a small grin playing at his mouth.

Her smile widened. "Well then, Newson, we're going to have some fun ... Jake's Corner style. Strap on your leather and let's go."

* * *

Eve pushed aside the door to the shed, turned on the light by pulling on the chain hanging down from the ceiling and illuminated a pair of dirt bikes. "They're old but they work just fine," she told Dane.

"I hope I can say the same thing about myself," he laughed. "It's been years since I've been on one of these things."

She was glad he'd been so willing to take them out for a ride. She had been dreading the evening alone with him. Short of hiding in her bedroom, there would have been no way to avoid his company.

Not that she didn't like his company. She liked it far too much for her own good. She'd given up hope of Stanley and Gilbert returning any time soon. She had hoped they could all do something as a group so she wouldn't have to worry about warding off Dane's advances all evening. She almost pitied Frank — whatever scheme Stanley and Gilbert had concocted to keep him away so long was obviously working.

They filled the gas tanks, checked the oil and pushed the bikes out into the moonlight. Minutes later they were racing along a trail through the bush.

Eve had considered taking him to see Lake of the Wolves. It was her favourite place to ride to, but he might see the lodge and that would naturally lead to questions she didn't want to answer. Instead she decided to take him to Jake's hunting shack, which was about an hour's ride.

She considered herself a fairly accomplished rider, thanks primarily to Stanley's antics. In the beginning, he had scaled back his daredevil riding skills until she had mastered control of the bike, but once satisfied she could handle herself, there'd been no mercy. Now she was as wild a rider as either Stanley or Gilbert.

She glanced over at Dane riding beside her. It was obvious he had spent many a day in his youth on a motorbike because he rode like he'd been born on it. She wondered just how sharp his skills still were as the trail came to a fork. She faced her bike so that her headlight illuminated the trail she wanted to ride. He pulled up beside her, engine revving. She gave him a sly grin. "Right or left?"

"Where do they go?"

"Same place. One's shorter and for old folks with bad backs. The other is a bit ... challenging." It wasn't really a lie, just a gross understatement. She bit back a smirk.

He laughed. "I don't suppose you want to take the one for old folks?"

"Not a chance!" she yelled and slipped the bike into gear, roaring off down the trail. She heard his laughter in the wind. She laughed out loud herself, invigorated by the cold night frost.

The trail was too narrow to ride side by side, and as Eve rounded a sharp corner, she yelled back a warning even though he probably couldn't hear anyway, "Get ready to fly!" The path dipped about four feet and then swelled again to another six feet before disappearing completely, sending her airborne. She landed on her front tire, bracing the bike with a leg while the back tire landed and skidded wildly beneath her, and then she revved the engine, easily scaling the next hill. She wondered, as she continued to race along the trail, how Dane was managing behind her, but he neatly clipped past her, pushing through the bush and stirring up a flurry of dried leaves in front of her.

It was her turn to follow and the wilder the ride, the faster Dane went. He was as hard to keep up with as Stanley. Determined not to be outdone, Eve took advantage of her knowledge of the trail and broke through the bush where it thinned a little and tried to overtake him, her bike at top speed, branches striking her helmet and whipping the leather gloves on her hands. She had nearly hit the trail ahead of him, but he manoeuvred around her when she had slowed slightly to cut in. She could hear his howl of triumph as she was forced to pull in behind him and follow him to the end of the trail, the bush being too thick to risk passing again.

As soon as they neared their destination and the path opened into a clearing, she cranked her handle to increase her speed and whipped by him. Her victory was short lived as he raced along beside her and edged her towards the bush. She laughed out loud, dropped her speed and cut in behind him but couldn't regain her lead. He skidded to a halt just short of Jake's shanty, whipping his bike around to face her as she pulled up in front of him.

His smile was wide with his victory as he removed his helmet. "Good grief! If that's how a woman takes a guy out on a date in Jake's Corner, what happens when they're engaged?"

Eve laughed, climbing off her bike and shaking her hair free of her helmet before pulling off her gloves. "You should see the weddings!"

"No," he groaned as he lifted himself off and stretched out his kinks, "I think I should see a chiropractor."

"Aha!" she replied. "I knew you were an old guy with a bad back."

"I might not have been before but I think I am now!" Dane chuckled and followed her to the bench sitting against the shack, stiffly lowering himself beside her.

She offered him a sip of water from the canteen she'd brought along.

"How many dates with Stanley did it take for you to learn to ride like that?" he asked in-between sips, then passed it back.

She paused to take a sip, trying not to think about his lips having just been where hers were now. She gave him a crooked smile. "Fishing, Dane?"

His own smile was just as crooked. "Absolutely."

She leaned against the shack. "I never actually dated Stanley."

"And Gilbert?"

She smiled down at her boots. Was there a tinge of jealousy in his voice? "We saw each other for a while. That's why Stanley had to teach me to ride. Gilbert was too afraid I'd hurt myself."

He looked like he wanted to ask more. She took pity on him. "Dating Gilbert was a bit like dating a brother ... now we're all just good friends."

He didn't say anything; instead he stared up at the stars, lost in his own thoughts. For a moment it looked as if he was going to comment but then appeared to change his mind.

They remained quiet on the bench, drinking in the night sky and the cold air, their breath misting around them.

"So, Just-Eve," he said, finally breaking the

silence and smiling over at her, "do you have a last name?"

She giggled. She had forgotten that he didn't know her name. "It's Barron," she said. "Eve Barron." She liked his smile when he gave it for his own sheer pleasure, when he wasn't seducing her with it. She smiled back.

He resumed watching the sky and then turned to her, his eyes twinkling in the moonlight. "Elliot."

"Pardon me?"

"I figured I should reciprocate and tell you my middle name."

She laughed and said his full name. "Dane Elliot Newson."

"What's yours?"

"My what?"

"Your full name."

"A woman has to have a few secrets, Dane Elliot Newson," she teased.

"Ah, yes, I agree," he replied, his eyes locking into hers, his grin still teasing. "I like a woman of mystery, but I do believe, Eve, you have a few more secrets than most."

"Is that so bad?" she said lightly.

"On the contrary," he answered softly and leaned closer to her. "I find it quite intriguing."

He was going to kiss her. Involuntarily she leaned away from him and put a hand to his chest.

Seeing her uncertainty, he took hold of her hand and kissed it. "I have a much younger brother who settled down into a rather ordinary suburban lifestyle," he murmured into her fingers. "When we were kids, my father left my mother for a younger woman, siring two half-sisters, and although my mother is still single, she is quite happy."

He reached for her other hand and pressing them

both between his, continued softly, "I have a Master's Degree in Commerce. After graduating, I worked for a small investment firm, living like a miser and saving every nickel I earned until I had enough to buy into a small laundromat business, which I have since gifted to my mother. And from there things just grew. There were pitfalls along the way, but I learned from my mistakes and built the company into the money machine it is today."

Shivers ran from her fingers to her toes as he turned up the palms of her hands and pressed his lips to each, the cold forgotten.

"I've never smoked cigarettes or anything else, I rarely get drunk, but I do eat red meat and anything else supposedly not good for me. I love jazz clubs, a really good restaurant and have travelled extensively, usually on business. I find the social commitments that come with my lifestyle a bore, but I do give generously to charities. Sometimes my work requires a certain ruthlessness, but I have never swindled anyone; I don't lie or cheat on my taxes, business or personal, and I adore my half-sisters to death. My word is my bond; if I give it, you can depend on it."

He raised his eyes to hers. "Do you know me now?"

All response dried up in her mouth, and Eve found her lips parting before his own had touched them, his mouth tender and almost comforting. Need for him exploded within her, her soul aching for his love. He released her hands, and she wrapped her arms around his strong shoulders, murmuring his name as he kissed first her throat and then her closed eyes. Their lips briefly found each other again, his hands immersed in her hair, his fingers twisting through its strands. As his mouth traced kisses down her neck, his name poured out from her lips once more.

Dane breathed a pleased chuckle into her ear and whispered, "At least this time you know my name."

He shifted ever so slightly away from her, placed a finger over her lips and smiled into her eyes. "Let's get back," he suggested, reaching for her hand and twisting her fingers through his, pressing a kiss to the tip of her nose. "As much as I'd like to stay here and kiss you all night, you're too precious to keep out here in the freezing cold."

Dane had called her precious. No one had ever called her that before. She marvelled at the delight of it as he gave her a solid parting kiss before pulling her to her feet.

She didn't want to return to the *Gas and Grill* and the worries about the lodge. Out here, away from it all, it didn't seem to matter whether or not Dane could be trusted. She thought about telling him that Jake kept dry firewood inside the shack and that there were even a couple of sleeping bags to help keep them warm. But it was only a thought, a wish that abandoning herself to him would cost nothing, that the outside world wouldn't be there to bring them trouble in the morning.

They climbed onto their bikes in silence, Eve feeling cold outside his embrace. "You set the pace," he said, motioning for her to precede him down the trail, and she couldn't help but think he was referring to more than just the ride back.

NINE

Dane lay on his back, resting his head in his hands and staring up at the yellow water stains on the ceiling, willing sleep to come. He held up his watch. Two a.m. He wondered if Eve was asleep. He grinned. She probably slept like a rock. She was too stubborn not to.

He punched the pillow into a more comfortable shape and tried to force himself to think about something else besides Eve and the taste of her lips or the desire in her eyes or the feel of her body against his.

He'd never known a woman like her, and it had taken all of the willpower he possessed to drive back to the *Gas and Grill* instead of carrying her into that hunting shack and making love to her until dawn. She wouldn't have argued against it — of that he was certain — at least not until morning when the regrets began to roll in. He'd never desired a woman more, and he had a strong sense that if he ever did possess her, he'd never want to let her go.

Maybe that was why he couldn't stand the thought of her coming to regret having been with him. He sensed within her, for reasons he could only guess at, a fear of him, and since he hadn't really done anything to earn her trust, it would have been only natural for her to reject him in the light of day.

Dane rolled onto his back again and asked himself with a disparaging grin when he'd developed this sudden chivalry. He almost laughed out loud when he recalled having called her precious. Where had he gotten a word like that?

Dane groaned and sat up, his bare feet scarcely noticing the cold floor beneath them, and wondered if he could remember how to hot-wire a truck. He was losing his mind.

If he was smart, he'd get the heck out of here, or before he knew it, it would be six kids and ten years later before someone from his office in Toronto finally tracked him down, only to find him wandering about Jake's Corner behind Stanley and Gilbert, eyes glazed and mumbling things like *yep* and *eh?* and babbling about what a great guy Jake was.

He grabbed his jeans from the foot of the bed and shoved his strong legs into them. Standing up, he pulled the zipper closed and wandered over to the window. He raised his arms and leaned against the window frame, his fingers drumming impatiently.

He asked himself if part of this attraction to Eve was that she gave him an excuse for prolonging his return to Toronto. He was relieved it was over with Vanessa, but he had felt her absence nonetheless. Loneliness was a new feeling. Or if he had been lonely before, he hadn't recognized it as such.

He tried to recall what had attracted him to Vanessa in the first place. Yes, she was beautiful but why did that now seem not enough? Had they ever shared any fun times together like he and Eve had tonight? Sure, there'd been ski trips and exotic vacations but he couldn't recall a time of sheer, spontaneous enjoyment.

In fact, at this moment he could scarcely remember what Vanessa was like. Hard and cold seemed to be the words which came to mind, and when had he come to think of her in those terms? Only since having experienced Eve's warmth, he was certain.

He chuckled as he pictured Eve crashing through the bush on her dirt bike, determined to overtake him, ignoring the branches swiping at her helmet and legs. And the way she had cleared that first jump like a hardened daredevil! He imagined she rode the snowmobiles just as recklessly, and yet, he had no trouble picturing her gliding smoothly through a crowd of his business associates, dressed to kill and thoroughly literate in world affairs.

She was neither hard nor cold. Soft, warm, kind, generous. And irresistibly wild. That was Eve. He envied Stanley and Gilbert's friendship with her, especially Gilbert, and he again wondered if Gilbert had ever shared her bed, then decided that he never wanted to know the answer to that.

He grabbed a pair of socks from his once-expensive-but-now-worthless suitcase and sat on the bed, his hands between his knees, twirling the socks absently. He might be sleeping across the hall right now if Eve hadn't practically locked herself in her room when they'd returned to the *Gas and Grill*.

The ride back had been uneventful. She had chosen the shorter, gentler route, ignoring him the whole way, and had spared him only a few brief glances while they stowed the bikes back in the storage shed. Although she did turn to him at the back door to the kitchen and stare so deeply into his eyes that he was sure she'd seen clear to his soul. "Dane ..." she had said, as if she had wanted to unburden herself and confess the details of the plot brewing at Jake's Corner. But then her face had changed along with her mind and she'd turned away, murmuring, "Never mind ..." under her breath before heading up the stairs without a backward glance.

As he'd watched her retreat, he'd considered following her and sweeping her off her feet before she reached her room, but where would that have gotten him? The same regrets in a warmer place, that's all.

He gave the socks a shake and they unpaired. He slipped one over a foot. So what, now? Launch a great seduction assault until she gave him what he wanted? And precisely what did he want? he asked himself as he pulled out a sweatshirt. A fast fling before he got out of here?

A fast fling wasn't entirely out of the question, but he intuitively knew Eve's passionate nature wouldn't permit her to enter into it detached and purely sexual, and when he left Jake's Corner, he'd leave behind a broken heart. And furthermore, she had a way about her that wouldn't allow you to get away unscathed yourself. He already knew he'd never forget her.

Shirt on, he crossed back to the window and stared out into the night. The moon was high. Maybe he'd go for a walk, or maybe he'd make a pot of coffee and do one of those crossword puzzles Eve always seemed to be passing the time with.

He expelled a deep, burdened sigh and laughed almost bitterly. The great, immune Dane Newson had been reduced to a mindless romantic idiot in the wilderness by a simple country girl. He grinned as he watched the tiny headlights of a vehicle appear in the distance. Eve was far from simple and he had serious doubts that she was entirely *country*, but most of all, she was the farthest thing from a *girl*.

The vehicle on the horizon drew closer and then drove on past Jake's Corner, making him wish for a moment that he was in that vehicle and on his way out of here. There was no point lying to himself. He wasn't sticking around Jake's Corner to play an entertaining game of strategy with Stanley and Gilbert, although he had to admit it was fun. He was sticking around to be with Eve and was damn glad he was *stranded*. He knew he should try to find a reason to move on to Foster Rapids or get back to the corporate jungle, but the thrill of the hunt had veered away from scoring the next business deal and, almost without his permission, focused itself exclusively on Eve.

Yes, she had everyone at Jake's Corner cross-eyed, including himself. He combed a hand through his streaked hair and crossed back to the bed, wondering if she wore a nightie when she slept. He wondered ...

Dane grabbed the three-day-old financial newspaper from underneath his suitcase and flipped it open in irritation. He didn't want to know what he wondered. Wondering certain things about Eve didn't make it easier to sleep.

* * *

Eve stretched and yawned. Sunlight rebelliously squeezed beneath the window blind, permeating the room with streams of bright yellow. She hadn't slept well but she'd slept late. She sunk further into the covers. Did she really have to endure another day of cat-and-mouse with Dane while constantly reliving his kisses every time she looked at him?

And Dane Newson certainly knew how to kiss a woman. He'd taught her that again last night, and over and over in her dreams. She flushed at the memory of her dreams and pulled the covers over her head, trying to block him out, but threw them off again, knowing it was an exercise in futility.

She had known that first instant when Dane had climbed out of his truck and flashed those green eyes and irresistible dimples that he possessed the ability to completely undo the promises she'd made to herself after leaving Bryce. She hadn't promised to never fall in love again, but she had vowed that if she ever did fall in love again, she would do so wisely, choosing her mate carefully and not allowing herself to be blinded by charm, success or a handsome face.

She laughed inwardly. It sounded so evolved ... but she'd already blown it. Her feelings for Dane were so strong and so sudden and so reminiscent of how hard she'd fallen for Bryce, it was quite possible she was falling in love with an illusion again!

She yanked the pillow from beneath her head and held it tightly over her face with a frustrated moan. There ... she admitted it. She *might be falling in love* with Dane Newson.

She might also be a fool, she remonstrated, and no more mature than when she'd foolishly married Bryce against everyone's wishes, particularly her father's.

Her father had taken one look at Bryce, pronounced him a scoundrel and said he doubted the marriage would last a year. Eve had stubbornly tried to hold the marriage together for five, but in the end she had to admit that her father's appraisal of Bryce had been accurate.

Now here she was, four years later and not the least bit wiser. At twenty-eight a woman should have herself sorted out.

She tossed the pillow to the floor and stared up at her ceiling. Hers was the only room in the place without water stains. She sighed deeply. What if

Dane was all that he claimed to be? What if she really could trust him? The thought might have made her giddy if thoughts to the contrary didn't also demand answers. Was she supposed to make a decision? She didn't want to decide. What if she chose wrongly, what then? Was there no other answer?

Perhaps there were no answers period, she decided, forcing herself out of bed, not wanting to think about it anymore. Perhaps, if she were lucky, life would just take its course and whatever was for the best would come to pass.

* * *

Dane's door was closed when Eve finally ventured out of her room and was still closed when she tiptoed out of the bathroom, dressed and combing her wet hair.

"Good morning!"

She jumped at the sound of his voice. He was standing at the top of the stairs, wearing a brilliant smile above a sweatshirt and jeans. The man in her dreams.

He glanced down at his wristwatch and then gave her a wry grin. "Sleep well?"

"Yes," she said lightly, shyly meeting the eyes that had haunted her through the long night.

"Me, too, but not quite so well as you, I'm afraid." He laughed softly and then drifted into silence.

They stared at each other, unspoken words suspended between them. Would it have been so terrible to have spent the night with him at the hunting shack? Would being lovers have dissipated her fears? And what about Dane? Once he'd had her, what then? Love her and leave her? Was it only in her dreams that she could safely love him?

Dane cleared his throat and indicated the stairs. "I've made coffee," he said, sounding uncertain of himself.

"Mmm ... good," she replied, words still stuck in her throat.

He made a wide sweep with his arm to show he expected her to lead the way.

She obliged him, averting her eyes as she slipped past and descended the stairs.

The tension between them was not lessened by being in the restaurant. She poured herself a cup of coffee and sat down across from him. They stared at each other over the rims of their cups as they sipped in silence.

"Eve," Dane said finally, his voice hushed as he reached over and began tracing lines along her fingers where they cupped her mug. "I lied to you. I didn't sleep at all. I've been up drinking coffee most of the night."

She stopped sipping, unable to confess her own sleepless hours, but she permitted her eyes to stay with his.

"Eve, I think we have something here, you and I." He gave a short laugh, his green eyes almost embarrassed. "I think I'm a really great guy, and I wish you'd give me a chance to prove it to you."

She lowered her eyes and her coffee mug, leaving behind the touch of his hand. Was this what she wanted? she asked, as she stared at a cigarette burn in the table top, for Dane to prove he was everything he'd told her he was? What then, marriage? Did she want to marry again? Maybe Dane wasn't the marrying kind. Would he, like Bryce, chase every skirt that caught his eye? No doubt that in the social circles Dane walked there was an endless supply of beautiful women.

How would she know, and not just hope, that she could trust him? And how would this great proof come to pass with him living in Toronto and her in Jake's Corner?

Moreover, the issue of the lodge was hanging over their heads. How would Dane feel about having been duped by everyone at Jake's Corner, including her? Would he still want to prove what a great guy he was after learning that? She wouldn't blame him if he high-tailed it out of here, bought into the lodge with Frank Loewen and let them all starve to death.

Maybe he would do that anyway, regardless of how he felt about her. Bryce had been coldly ruthless when it came to closing a deal. *There's no right or wrong in business*, he'd always say, *just weak and strong*.

"Eve," Dane said quietly, interrupting her confused thoughts and placing a hand over hers, "I'm not asking you to make any great commitment; I'm asking you to trust me just a little. If I turn out to be a scumbag, you can send me packing anytime you want and I'll go."

She raised her eyes, searching the earnestness in his, then dropped them again as a deep regret filled her heart. Perhaps she'd misjudged Dane Newson based solely on appearances. Maybe he wasn't like Bryce at all. She sighed with the burden of her guilt. How could she possibly tell him about the lodge?

"Here come your cohorts," Dane said, referring to Stanley and Gilbert who were pulling up to the *Gas and Grill*, Stanley in the tow truck, Gilbert driving Dane's rented vehicle.

Dane lifted her chin so that she would look at him. He gave her a soft smile. "I won't pressure you. Think about it for a while."

She nodded her head and closed her eyes. Obviously life wasn't going to make the decision for her as she'd hoped.

* * *

Dane knew he hadn't been able to reach her. Whatever troubled her heart still had too great a grip on her. He envied Stanley and Gilbert anew as he watched them climb out of their truck and surmised their easy-going relationship with Eve was likely due to the fact that they demanded nothing from her.

There had to have been a Mr. Barron at one time; it was the only explanation for Eve's resistance, and he'd have to have been a helluva brute. How could anyone hurt something as precious as Eve? There was that word again. He grinned as Stanley and Gilbert entered the *Gas and Grill*; he'd undeniably joined the ranks of the potty-headed folk at Jake's Corner.

"Hey, Dan!" Gilbert said with a gleaming grin. "We've checked your truck all over and she's fit for the road. Heck, now that we've looked after her, she's even better than before."

"So you're free to leave anytime," his partner added from behind and with a gleam of his own.

"You can leave right now," Gilbert said. "In fact, she's got gas, the weather is good and you'll get there in plenty of time for your important meeting. We even got your cell phone working."

Dane laughed as Gilbert tossed it to him. His meeting was two days ago. "I can't thank you guys enough for your help." He'd used the word *help* rather loosely; *obstruction* was a more apt description of what these two jokers had done as far as getting him to Foster Rapids went.

"Only thanks we need is either cash or a cheque," Stanley chortled, making his way to the coffee pot and filling two mugs, "preferably cash."

"I think we can work something out," Dane replied smoothly, not surprised the conversation had, after two days, finally gotten around to the discussion of money. "I'll straighten things out with the insurance company when I return the vehicle."

"Well, that's that then!" Eve exclaimed, jumping up from her chair and tossing him a blatantly artificial smile as Stanley came up behind her with a coffee for Gilbert. "I'll throw together a few sandwiches for you, and you can be on your way. It shouldn't take more than a minute or two."

"I'd appreciate that," Dane said as he rose from the table, accepting the keys Gilbert held out to him before heading towards the stairs.

It was plain Eve was anxious to see him leave. She went straight to the kitchen and immediately set to work, banging utensils and slamming drawers in her customary fashion.

Climbing the stairs, Dane berated himself for having moved too quickly with her. She reminded him of a little bird, stopping just out of reach and resting long enough for you to fool yourself into thinking you might actually catch her, but as soon as you reached out, away she flew. Now she'd be leery of letting him get even remotely close to her.

He decided the three pots of coffee he'd consumed over the past six hours had addled his brains. He'd learned long ago, when negotiating deals, to let his quarry come in real close before pouncing. He'd clearly misjudged how ready Eve had been.

He closed his bedroom door, pulled the bed away from the wall and plugged in his laptop. No email from Diane yet. It was possible that the wacky antics of the people at Jake's Corner was truly the norm and he was the crazy one. It was also possible that everything that had occurred was coincidental.

He sent Diane another message anyway. Might as well confirm whether or not there had indeed been a Mr. Barron in Eve's life; it might help him figure out a way to catch her. He could see it in her eyes and feel it when he kissed her that she wanted him to catch her. She was just too afraid to let him.

He'd come to the conclusion during his long night of crossword puzzles that since he knew Eve was a rare find, he'd be a fool to walk away from her. Precisely what that meant, he had no idea, but he was hooked. So hooked that he wanted to cart her off with him to Toronto, kicking and screaming the whole way if he had to. So hooked the big "M" word had actually been on his mind once or twice. He unplugged his computer. Okay, more than once or twice. He'd even pictured little reproductions of Eve running around.

He laughed out loud. How was it possible to feel so strongly about a woman in so short a time? Was this what falling in love did to a man?

It was preposterous, really, and yet he knew without a doubt that if she gave him the chance he was asking for — the time to really get to know one another — they would become more vital to each other's existence than the air they breathed.

He laughed at himself again. He was losing his mind. What did he know about love or marriage for that matter? It was time to take his partner and likely only true friend, Nelson Adsum, to a hockey game and poll him about the whole thing. What was the secret behind the kind of love he and his wife, Anna, never seemed to run out of?

Of course, he couldn't just openly grill Nelson.

He'd have to bury it in the conversation, since Nelson had a nose for stuff like that. With Dane's luck, he'd sniff it out and bust a gut laughing.

"One day, Newson, you're gonna fall, and you're gonna fall harder than any of those creeps in the boardroom, and when you do, old buddy," Nelson would snort whenever Dane had happened to comment on his almost slavish devotion to Anna, a source of constant jibes among the less dedicated married men on staff, "I'm gonna be there right behind you, laughing my head off."

Dane smirked to himself as he snapped his suitcase shut and did the best he could with his briefcase. It truly was laughable. The sane thing to do would be to head south to Toronto immediately and ignore any and all calls from Frank Loewen in case it tempted him to think about passing through Jake's Corner again.

He surveyed the barren space that had been his home for the last two nights. It wouldn't be too difficult to just up and leave since he didn't care in the least anymore about getting to Foster Rapids or buying a lodge. Hell, at this moment he didn't care about the sole focus of his life, Newson Enterprises. Yeah, it would be pretty easy to head off to Toronto without so much as a backwards glance ... if he could pluck and transplant that dark-eyed wildflower otherwise known as Eve.

Dane picked up his luggage, shoving his briefcase under his arm, and made his way downstairs where his three conspirators waited for him at a table. At least the two-hour drive to Foster Rapids would give him time to clear his head. He needed to make a few decisions.

Stanley greeted him with a toothy smile and stood up to shake his hand. "It's been nice knowin' ya,

Dan."

"Likewise," Dane replied, giving the young man's hand a firm grip.

"Glad we could help you out," Gilbert commented, reaching overtop of Eve to extend his hand as well.

"How much do I owe you?" Dane asked.

Gilbert and Stanley exchanged glances. "Call it our good deed for the week," Gilbert said.

"Yes, I agree. Consider yourself our guest," Eve piped in and pushed a paper bag towards him. "We're just glad to help a stranger out."

Dane picked up the bag, smiling at her eagerness to relegate him to the status of a guest, a far cry from her response to him last night. It also confirmed the wisdom in not having slept with her. He couldn't imagine the state she'd have herself in now if he had. "I appreciate your hospitality," he said to them all but looking at Eve. "You've all been exceedingly generous, helpful and kind to the point of being beyond even friendship."

Eve coloured ever so slightly and cleared her throat. She had understood his implication. "We aim to do our best."

"Think nothin' of it!" Stanley added.

"Hey, it's the least we could do," Gilbert affirmed, slapping Dane on the back and nudging him towards the door. "We better not keep you from wasting any more time."

"Yes, the day goes fast up here," Stanley said. "Seems like you've just rolled out of bed and before you know it, the sun's settin' again."

"The weather changes fast, too," Gilbert continued, nudging him some more. "One minute it's calm and sunny and the next thing you know, a storm rolls in."

"Gilbert's right," Eve added with a nod of her

brown head, following behind Stanley. "The weather is very unpredictable."

"You wouldn't want to waste any time getting to Foster Rapids," Stanley told him.

Dane grinned at the three of them. Interludes of sanity at Jake's Corner had occurred only during the times he and Eve had been alone. Once Stanley, Gilbert, Jake or anyone else came into the mix, chaos erupted, and now it was blatantly obvious that they wanted him gone, and quickly.

He entertained the thought of sticking around, just to see what lengths they'd go to in order to get him out of the way of whatever was going on. His grin widened. He'd stop in on the way back. By that time, if there was anything to know about these queer folks, Diane would have apprised him of it.

He climbed inside his truck, Stanley holding the door open for him while he tossed in his cases. He started up the engine, closed the door and rolled down the window. "Thanks again. I'll stop in on my way back."

Eve gave him a tight smile. "Sure, that'd be great," she said, but he could tell she hoped he wouldn't.

Dane put the truck into gear.

"Aw, don't bother," Stanley said with a wave of his hand. "We know you got more important business than jawing over coffee with us. Just drive on by if you don't need gas."

"See ya, man!" Gilbert called out as Dane pulled away from them.

Dane drove up onto the approach to the highway, shaking his head. Had he really lived the past two days, or had it been some kind of waking nightmare? In his rear view mirror, he could see Eve standing by the gas pumps, Stanley and Gilbert waving behind her. Eventually, the shrinking view disappeared altogether, leaving him longing for what his eyes were already missing.

No doubt about it. He would definitely stop in on his way back.

TEN

Dane's truck vanished into the horizon while Gilbert and Stanley congratulated themselves with hearty slaps on the back and then caught up Eve between them, lifting her off the ground with loud yelps of victory.

"We did it!" they exclaimed in unison before dropping her unceremoniously as the unmistakable sound of Jake's approaching *Sweet-Pea* heralded his arrival.

Shivering in the autumn wind, Eve watched them saunter off towards Jake, yelling anew, and told herself the tears beginning to trickle down her face were just the aftermath of two long, exhausting, roller-coaster days. She hugged her arms to herself and feigned checking the reservoir of window-washing water by the gas pumps.

"You fellers sent Frank to Iqaluit?" Jake's drawl could be heard as *Sweet-Pea*'s engine finally finished rumbling.

Eve welcomed the quiet laugh that briefly interrupted her tears. They'd shipped Frank off to Baffin Island?

"It doesn't take much of Harry Johnson's homemade whiskey to bring out a fella's deepest wishes," Stanley explained with a deep laugh.

"Lucky for us," Gilbert added, joining Stanley's laughter. "Frank shared his just before he passed out."

She couldn't help a small smile as she pictured Frank prostrate on Harry's sagging sofa, not an unfamiliar sight in Jake's Corner when the moonshine was uncorked. Someone always fell victim to the potent liquid and spent the night snoring on the sofa, blissfully ignorant of the party going on around him.

"Lucky thing also that Ben Orbanski happened to be in the neighbourhood," Gilbert said as Jake climbed out of *Sweet-Pea*. "Who knows, with any luck some bad weather will roll in and it'll be three days before they can get back."

Her anguish suspended by her astonishment, Eve dropped the wiper into the reservoir and stared at her friends. She wouldn't let an old lady cross the street with Ben, let alone send anyone up in a plane with him. He was the craziest daredevil of a bush pilot the North had ever seen, and everyone from Iqaluit to Whitehorse and all the way south to the U.S. border, and probably even then some, knew it. If you absolutely had to get something delivered in the worst of weather conditions, you sent Ben, but you sure as heck never actually got in a plane with him.

"How you fellers gonna explain this when he gets back?" Jake asked, stretching out a crick in his back.

"We'll just say it was drunken fun," Gilbert continued. "His car's already back in Foster Rapids. Stanley and I drove it there last night. What can he really accuse of us? Besides, he's getting off easy. He's our only suspect as to who filed the environmental complaint, and the more I think about it, the more I think maybe Loewen had all this planned even before he offered to lend us money."

Eve was shocked. For lack of any other suspect, it had crossed her mind that Frank might have filed the environmental complaint, but it had made little sense until now.

"Heh, heh!" Stanley laughed. "I haven't had that much fun since Elijah Spence's stag party when we put him on the bus to Thompson. Remember that, Eve?" he called out across the lot.

She couldn't help another quiet laugh and a small grin which she hoped masked her misery. Elijah's fiancée, Edna, had been so upset that she made everyone jump into their vehicles and all race to catch up to the bus. It had been an amazing sight to see five or six vehicles surrounding the bus on the highway, forcing it to halt so that she could rescue her hapless man.

Their wedding had been the most fun Eve could remember having at such an event. But then, all she had to compare it with were the stuffy, pretentious affairs she'd suffered through with Bryce, of which her own had been no exception. A chill snaked through her at the memory of their life together, and she found herself longing for the warmth of Dane's kisses.

Unbidden and needing no more prompting than the mere thought of him, two solitary tears slid from Eve's eyes and rolled down her face, one pausing on her lip. She wiped it away and inspected the gas hoses for signs of wear. She should be thankful for the turn of events, she consoled herself. Hadn't she hoped that somehow life would just take things into its own hands and work out what was for the best?

Whatever Stanley and Gilbert's reasons for sending Dane off in such a hurry, she knew they hadn't considered, nor had she realized it herself until it was too late, that even with Frank out of the picture for a few days, Dane would most certainly return from Foster Rapids armed with the truth about Lake of the Wolves and accusing them all of deceit, kidnapping and who-knew-what-else.

The communities up here were awfully small. Everyone knew everyone else's business. Frank Loewen wasn't necessarily the only one who could apprise Dane of the story. All it would take is a curious waitress pouring him coffee and asking *what brought him to this neck of the woods* and the next thing, someone would overhear and start filling his ears.

He'd hate her, she was sure of it now, and although she'd convinced herself all along that if she never saw him again it wouldn't matter, the truth had now been painfully exposed. It did matter, but the revelation had come too late.

"By that time we'll have gotten funding from the Band Council," Gilbert was saying.

"... and who cares, anyway, what Loewen thinks," Stanley put in.

"Yer certain they'll give it to you?" Jake asked, his hoarse voice skeptical as he made his way alongside them towards the doors of the *Gas and Grill*.

"They're voting on it this morning, and the word around is that they think it would be good for everyone if the lodge remained in the hands of the community," Gilbert replied, mounting the steps.

"I think yer countin' yer chickens before they're even eggs," Jake puffed as his ancient legs mounted the steps.

"People around here are practically busting with the news and there'll be lots of celebrating going on after the vote. The Band Council moved a lot faster on this issue than we expected. That's why we got rid of Newson so quickly; we didn't want him getting wind of it and maybe messing things up."

"He's no fool," Stanley put in, holding the door open for Jake, "and might not be too happy to discover he'd been played for one. Plus, this way he can't accuse us of nothin'. We figure, even if it falls through, which it won't, when he can't find Loewen in Foster Rapids, he'll just head back to Toronto. That'll buy us time to figure out something else."

"Hey, Eve, come celebrate," Stanley called out before their voices trailed away and the door closed hard behind them.

Eve replaced the gas nozzle on the pump as fresh tears grew in her eyes now that they could safely fall free. She should be overjoyed that they'd salvaged the lodge, but their deceit had cost her Dane. She should have told him everything last night, but she hadn't been able to bring herself to do it. For him to hear it from someone else ... the thought of his eyes cold and hard towards her brought the swift sting of tears again.

She wiped them away and took a deep breath. Perhaps this was the way it was meant to be. Maybe fate had spared her many years of the same kind of heartache Bryce had put her through. She loitered by the pumps a few moments longer until she was certain her tears were under control, then went inside and presented a composed facade to the three men seated in her restaurant. She'd do the rest of her crying later.

* * *

Foster Rapids Welcomes You to the Best Darn Fishin' in the World!

Dane smiled as he read the sign boasting an indeterminate fish and guarding the entrance to a raggle-taggle town perched haphazardly over the rocks from which it had been carved. It was a teeming metropolis in comparison to Jake's Corner and had the appearance of a typical, isolated mining town until you spied the plywood covering the storefront windows of merchants now long gone.

He drove along Main Street, deciding it must be the requisite name of every main street in every small town in the world. Noting one closed business after another, he pulled into the sole surviving gas station and, turning on his cellular phone, dialed Diane's number at the office.

"I knew it would be you," she responded laughingly to his greeting.

He smiled into the phone, surprised at how comforting a familiar voice could be. "So, has my overpaid assistant done her homework yet?"

"Overworked is closer to the truth," she drawled. "Which tidbit of news would you like first?"

"Surprise me."

"Well," Diane started, her tone warning that interesting information was about to come his way, "it's a fascinating coincidence that the people at Jake's Corner you asked me to investigate happen to also be the principals in a company called Lake of the Wolves Lodge Inc."

She gave him a minute to digest this information, and he needed it. He'd told himself he wouldn't be surprised by whatever he learned from Diane, but he hadn't been prepared to hear that Eve's buddies owned the lodge Frank Loewen had been trying to sell him. "Is Eve Barron involved as well?"

"I thought you'd never ask," Diane replied. "She was the titled owner of the land in question and sold it to the lodge for one hundred dollars. The land was sold to her by one Nehemiah Theophilus Jake for five dollars."

Dane was stunned. They'd played him for a fool. "What's Frank Loewen's involvement?" he managed to ask, rubbing his eyes, unable to believe he'd been duped by a pair of sultry brown eyes and a seductive smile.

"This is where it gets interesting," Diane said. "From what I can see, he's not involved at all, but my guess is he's their private financier. LOWL, that's my acronym for efficiency's sake, has no outstanding loans, mortgages or liens, but they had to have obtained financing from somewhere because the principals couldn't have had enough to build on their own."

"They might have sold shares," Dane suggested.

"They did, but only to local people who paid one hundred dollars each for a total of two hundred shares."

Dane did quick mental math. "That's only twenty-thousand dollars."

"And not enough to build the beautiful baby in the picture from your files."

"There's no outstanding mortgage? Was there ever one?"

"Nope," Diane confirmed. "Nothing."

Dane drummed his fingers against the steering wheel. If Loewen had lent them money, why wouldn't he have registered a mortgage against them?

"Want to hear something else?" She didn't wait for him to answer. "Sources tell us they did apply for a mortgage at several banks, but they were refused. Apparently nobody had faith in the project."

"How much were they asking for?"

"Five-hundred-thousand."

Dane whistled. It wasn't a lot in his world but it

would certainly be a lot for the crew at Jake's Corner.

"Yeah, it's a far cry from twenty," Diane said.

"What makes you think Loewen was the one to lend them money?" It was the same assumption he'd have made, but he knew Diane would have something more concrete than a hunch to back up her presumptions. He couldn't help a smile. Frank must've been the man he'd seen Stanley and Gilbert cart off into their truck.

"Frank Loewen is flat broke."

"Okay, let me guess, he is flat broke because he cashed in everything he had, totalling somewhere around five-hundred-thousand dollars, but the money's vanished."

"Something like that. There were three large chequing withdrawals from his account over the past two years."

"I suppose it's too much to ask who the cheques were made payable to?"

He could almost see Diane roll her eyes through the telephone. "I'm an extremely resourceful woman and damn good at what I do, Dane, but I'm not a miracle worker. You can't begin to know the favours you owe as payment for information I dug up for you, especially since you wanted it yesterday."

Dane grimaced. Most of the information Diane availed herself of was public domain and available to the person willing to do a little work, and while he permitted her to hire her own crew to do much of the leg work, she also had an army of external contacts eager to help her out in exchange for favours, usually in the form of charitable donations for pet causes or a trade of information. Some of her methods, he knew were only barely legal or less, but she'd say if people were in the habit of leaving information lying around, it was silly not to pick it up. She'd saved his neck more than once with a last-minute tidbit of data. The criminals she'd unearthed over the years were astounding.

Diane misinterpreted his silence and groaned, "All right, I'll find out who he gave the money to."

"No, no," Dane insisted. "It's not necessary. We know where the money went." Something about this story confused him, but he couldn't find the weak spot. He needed some time to sift through it all. He was still reeling from learning of Eve's involvement. He'd known they were up to something, but hadn't imagined it would be of this magnitude. They were much better con artists than he'd given them credit for, especially Stanley and Gilbert; he'd never been entirely convinced they were the dimwits they pretended to be, but he'd never have guessed this. As for Eve, he suspected her role was merely to be herself.

"And, Dane, about little Miss Barron?"

He braced himself. Diane's tone was ominous. "Guess who ex-hubby is."

"I'm afraid to ask."

"Bryce Barron of Barron Real Estate."

Dane nearly choked. "Barron Real Estate?"

"Yessiree, the one and only," Diane stated. "Filthy rich, lying cheat and notorious ladies' man. Cradle robber, too, if you want my opinion. She was eighteen when they married; he a mere forty-two. But all my sources say she had truly loved him. Go figure."

"How'd a mismatched pair like that hook up?"

"Who knows!"

"I know it's a shot in the dark," he said with heavy sarcasm, "but their marriage ended because of, oh I don't know, adultery, maybe?"

"Habitual."

"Doesn't Eve have money from her divorce?"

"He had so many women on the sly, she could have drained millions out of him, but supposedly she didn't want to fight him for it. She just wanted out regardless of what she lost, which was apparently everything. Do you want to know where she had lived?"

Dane groaned. "Not really, but I suppose you're going to tell me anyway."

"Of course," Diane laughed. "Picture the happy couple in their own little world on The Bridle Path."

Dane laughed at the mention of one of Toronto's most elite neighbourhoods. "I feel like a pauper in comparison."

"You are," Diane agreed.

"See, you are overpaid," he countered.

Dane rubbed his neck and tried to picture Eve married to Bryce Barron. Somehow he just couldn't imagine it. Gilbert was one thing, but Bryce Barron? A creep like him wouldn't know what to do with a woman like her. "All right," he said to Diane, sorting his thoughts, "see if you can find out what's not fitting in this puzzle, and I'll get back to you tomorrow before I track down Frank Loewen."

"Sure thing boss," Diane replied. "Get some rest, you sound exhausted. Oh, I almost forgot ..."

"What?"

"I don't want to point out a serious blunder on your part, but just how closely did you look at the map before you left Toronto?"

"Obviously not as close as you think I should have. What did I miss?"

"Lake of the Wolves is only forty kilometres from Jake's Corner."

"Why am I not surprised?"

"I don't know boss," Diane chuckled, "but you could have saved yourself a long drive if you'd known where you were going."

Dane hung up, shaking his head. He'd track Loewen down tomorrow; he was in no mood to discuss business with the man right now. He assessed the imaginatively named Foster Rapids Hotel across the street, suddenly longing for his lumpy bed across the hall from Eve. It was going to be another sleepless night.

* * *

Eve leaned on the handle of the buffer and gloated over the sparkling kitchen before her. Okay, so maybe sparkling was an exaggeration, but the floor did gleam and the old, stainless-steel sink and counters shone as much as they could through years of scratches. She'd had the *Gas and Grill* to herself the whole afternoon and had spent the first hour crying into her coffee cup. Eventually, she had commanded herself to master her tears and to work Dane out of her mind. So she had proceeded to the kitchen and declared war on the grease and grime which had been gradually building up when she hadn't been paying attention.

It had proved to be a therapeutic decision. The time scrubbing and scouring had provided an outlet for her sorrow and allowed her mind the freedom to wander, bringing her to the realization that, in her heart, she didn't truly believe that Dane was the same sort of scoundrel Bryce had been. She'd merely told herself that to keep from losing her head to him, a tactic which, unfortunately, had not been successful.

Somewhere in-between washing the windows and

stripping the floor, she'd arrived at the decision that if he returned from Foster Rapids still ignorant of the truth about the lodge, she'd take the risk of confessing everything to him. It wasn't as if she had anything to lose. And who knew, perhaps he'd forgive her for the deception. Perhaps he'd still want to give her a chance to get to know him better. After all, hadn't he hinted that he might not object to being kidnapped by her?

ELEVEN

He'd been told Frank Loewen's office was a little farther down the street, so Dane chose to walk the distance despite the brisk autumn wind which greeted him upon stepping outside. It had been a sleepless night as he had predicted, but his body appeared not to notice that it had been deprived of rest. He decided he was likely running on a combination of adrenalin and several pots of coffee.

Dane believed, with a few exceptions, he'd pieced together most of the puzzle regarding the mysterious lodge he'd been so unfortunate as to become entangled with. He just had a couple more questions and hoped to acquire the answers from Loewen.

He'd already decided he wouldn't go see the lodge itself. He was sick of travelling, but he'd explain to Frank that he was due back to Toronto and would have to take a look at the lodge on a second trip out.

He stopped in front of a door with *F.Loewen Properties* etched into the glass in block letters, twisted the handle and stepped inside.

"I knew you'd show up sooner or later," a short, roly-poly man bellowed at him from behind one of three desks, all of them vacant except his own.

"Frank Loewen at your service."

* * *

Eve wiped down the dirty tables the morning coffee-crowd had left behind, pausing occasionally for a nervous glance towards the road. She didn't expect Dane any time soon, but knew she'd be sitting on pins and needles until he finally pulled in for gas. Eve straightened a few chairs and dumped the stale coffee down the drain. She longed to relieve her tension with a walk in the crisp autumn air or a wild ride on a dirt bike, but she didn't dare risk missing Dane, knowing he might not want to wait around until she returned before continuing on to Toronto. She realized she didn't have his telephone number, his address or anything other than the name of his company, Newson Enterprises.

Thinking about Dane's telephone number and address reminded her that her own telephone was still unplugged. She used it so seldom, she'd forgotten all about it. She went behind the counter in the convenience store, opened the cupboard and plugged the phone back in, hoping, unlikely as it was, that she hadn't missed a call from Dane.

* * *

Dane was halfway back to Jake's Corner and still shaking his head in disbelief. Frank Loewen was as nutty as the crew at the *Gas and Grill*.

Frank had indeed been the poor sucker he'd seen abducted by Stanley and Gilbert. He had to give the boys credit for their scheme to ship him off to Iqaluit, but the wily Frank had slipped from their clutches when he'd sobered up just outside Churchill and bribed the pilot with two cases of whiskey plus expenses instead of the one case agreed to by Stanley and Gilbert. Now the pilot had three cases of whiskey, cash in his pocket and no assignment.

Frank had been more than happy to spill out the story of his kidnapping but was not so willing to disclose the whole truth regarding the lodge. However, when Dane pressed him regarding what possible motives Stanley and Gilbert could have had for kidnapping him, Frank admitted that they, along with Eve, were the current titled owners of the lodge.

"But when you contacted my office, you insisted that you were the owner," Dane had said.

"It's only a matter of time until I have the papers," Frank had explained. "It's impossible for them to repay me. So, technically speaking, I am the owner."

"How much do they owe you?"

Frank's reply had been evasive. "Well, that's private information that they don't want made public. I can't breach a confidence like that."

"What's the land appraised at?" Dane had asked, finally getting to the real question he wanted answered.

"I've got it right here," Frank had told him, withdrawing a folder from the filing cabinet behind him. "It's sitting at a net worth of five-hundred-thousand, and that's before you include the value of the lodge, which is nearly completed."

Dane had whistled, making a mental note of the appraising company's name and address. "That's a fair chunk of money." It wasn't but he had played along.

"It's a fair chunk of land, practically encircling the

lake. Fifteen-hundred acres in all."

Dane manoeuvred the truck around another pothole, nearly dropping the sandwich he'd bought from the hotel in Foster Rapids and been attempting to eat. *White bread, chicken and plenty of mayonnaise.* The visit with Loewen hadn't given him much new information other than to confirm that he was a slippery businessman, not too bright in the brains department and precisely the sort of man Dane avoided conducting business with. Men like Loewen lacked vision, and their loyalty came cheap. Lethal handicaps they were, as business associates, not only because they couldn't be trusted, but also because their huge egos deluded them into thinking they were financial wizards.

Diane was investigating the agency which had done the appraisal of the land. Something wasn't quite right. Why would Loewen risk his entire capital against the full equity of a property? Furthermore, why hadn't five-hundred-thousand dollars been enough to open the lodge? Yes, it was a beautiful piece of architecture according to the photos he'd seen, but it should have been sufficient financing. They must have run into a roadblock of some kind and been forced to stop building. It wouldn't be the first time he'd seen that happen.

A bright orange sun hovered over the horizon along the edge of the bush as the road veered towards the west, necessitating the use of his sunglasses. He slipped them on with a free hand, the other never leaving the steering wheel. The highway was still the most miserable piece of work he'd ever driven over, but he noticed it less and the vein of thought he'd been avoiding slipped back into his mind, and this time he didn't push it away.

As shocked and disappointed as he'd been to discover Eve's deceit, he supposed he couldn't really blame her. He saw now that it hadn't been easy for her to deceive him. It explained so much of her vacillating manner towards him, as if she were torn between an old loyalty and a desire for a new one.

The whole thing must have caught them all by surprise. It was obvious they hadn't known anything about Frank's plans for their lodge. And it was equally obvious that Frank had wanted to keep them in the dark about it, since he'd insisted Dane meet him in Foster Rapids, even though it would have made far more sense to hook up at Jake's Corner. Moreover, if he hadn't rolled his truck, they'd still all be in the dark. It was him shooting off his own mouth to Jake that had initiated the whole process and when he got to the crux of things, it had been him pursuing Eve. She had merely allowed him to, and even that had required some persuasion on his part.

He looked at his wristwatch. He'd make it to Jake's Corner in about an hour. He decided he'd tell her he knew about the lodge and ask her to fill in the empty blanks with a promise to help her out as much as he could. He wasn't sure he wanted to get tangled up with anyone over the lodge anymore. It appeared far too risky, and his shareholders would have a fit, but he wouldn't rule it out just yet. However, he was definitely not hooking up with F. Loewen Properties.

Dane chuckled to himself. He'd added his own twist to the plot before he left Foster Rapids. Dane smiled widely into the sunset. Loewen was probably already on the telephone to Toronto.

He sipped from the thermos of coffee he'd bought in Foster Rapids and asked himself for the hundredth time how the heck had Eve gotten herself involved with Frank Loewen. She must have been desperate for cash. Or maybe she was just a trusting woman. It would explain her marriage to Bryce Barron.

Now there was an unlikely match. No wonder it hadn't lasted. He'd run across Barron a few times over the years and never liked the man. He was too polished, (*suave*, Diane had said) and his business deals always seemed to land him in the newspapers over something controversial.

Dane tried to remember if he'd ever seen Eve on Bryce's arm, but there had been a different woman every time he'd seen him, each of them stunningly beautiful, and he'd never paid much attention to Bryce Barron anyway.

Dane pictured Eve standing next to Bryce and had to admit she wouldn't have looked out of place, although she didn't strike him as your average trophy wife, either. She must have made Barron's life hell at times because she wasn't the type to put up with a lot of nonsense.

Dane now understood the fear he'd seen in her eyes whenever she'd responded to his advances. She wanted him but no doubt feared he was just another Bryce. He smiled into the slowly darkening sky and opening his console, sorted through its contents. She couldn't be more wrong. However, winning her over was likely going to be the biggest challenge of his life. He sipped his coffee and slipped a new CD into the player. He was equal to the task.

* * *

The telephone was ringing again. This time Eve decided to answer it. It had rung several times during the past hour, and fearing it might be Dane, she had studiously ignored it. Her bravado had lessened as each hour had passed so that by evening, she had none left at all. Having the entire day to think about facing Dane had given her ample time to find reasons why she shouldn't.

She put down her pen and left the crossword puzzle. She'd have to face him sooner or later; perhaps over the telephone would be easiest. Perhaps if she told him about the lodge right now, his anger would be spent by the time he stopped for gas. It was on its tenth ring when she finally lifted the receiver.

"It's about bloody time," a woman's voice hissed in her ear. "Don't you people know that when a telephone rings, you're supposed to answer it? I thought this was a business number."

"It's answered now. What can I do for you?"

"I think your employer needs to know how rude you are," the woman stated impatiently. "Is this the *Last Chance Gas & Grill*?"

"Mmhmm," Eve answered, guessing the caller was one of Dane's office assistants. This one needed a crash course in *people skills*.

"Was that a yes?"

"Mmhmm."

"Can't you people speak? I'd heard you were isolated, but this is ridiculous. Is Dane Newson there?"

"Nope."

"Ah, she can speak," the woman snarled. "But he was there yesterday?"

"Mmhmm."

"Do you know where he is now?"

"Nope."

"Could you be just a bit more helpful, dear?" the woman asked. "I've been trying to locate my fiancé. I'd heard he had an accident and all I want to know is if he's all right. If you do see him again, if it's not too difficult for you, do you think you could remember to tell Mr. Newson to call his fiancée, Vanessa? That's V-A-N-E-S-S-A."

* * *

Dane's truck slowed at the corner and turned into the *Gas and Grill*. Eve went into the convenience store, determined he wouldn't get past the till. She was ready for him. She'd been waiting, like a sentry, one solid hour by the window.

He filled the gas tank himself and as if noticing the sun had set, pulled off his sunglasses, stuffed them into his shirt pocket, climbed the steps and opened the door. A wide dimpled grin and sparkling green eyes greeted her, but their power over Eve had died with Vanessa's phone call.

"You have a message," Eve announced curtly, shoving him a note.

Dane stared at it a moment. "Vanessa called? Why would she be calling?" He appeared perplexed but Eve wasn't fooled for a minute. Bryce had been able to don the most convincing act, on the spot, whenever he'd needed to. It was clear the man standing in front of her possessed the same gift also.

"I don't know, Dane," Eve sneered. "Isn't that something fiancées do when the person they're engaged to goes missing — call around looking for them?"

"My fiancée?" Dane asked, looking even more

perplexed. "Where would you get the idea that Vanessa is my fiancée?"

"You're denying it?"

"Of course, I'm denying it! I'm not engaged to anyone, nor have I ever been."

Eve wasn't the least bit surprised that Dane denied having a fiancée. Men of his ilk were all the same. She could write his script for him and he'd speak his lines word for word. "Naturally that's what you say now that you've been caught. I'll bet you play up to women everywhere you go while poor Vanessa sits around waiting for you, oblivious to what a cad you are. Perhaps I should call her and tell her that the only reason we haven't slept together is because I very wisely didn't trust you for an instant. I wonder what she'd think about the love of her life after that."

"I don't know what she'd bloody think!" Dane bit out in frustration. "She isn't my fiancée. Call her and ask her yourself."

"That's cute, Dane," Eve said, "but it's a little too late to call my bluff since she's already told me the wedding's this spring."

"Well, it's news to me," Dane ground out, raking his hands through his sun-streaked hair and pacing down the toiletries aisle. "Eve, believe me, Vanessa is not my fiancée. I don't know why she'd tell you that. We were seeing each other, that part is true, but it's over. It's been over for a while."

"Well, Dane, it's obvious you two have a serious communication problem. Either one of you is quite confused or one of you is a liar. Which is it?"

"There was no confusion," Dane insisted.

"So Vanessa is a liar?"

"I hate to think so," Dane replied.

Eve's laugh was brittle. "Oh that's rich, Dane. Now, we're going to blame the victim in all this."

Dane stopped pacing and reached for her hands, but she held them back. He let his hands fall to his side, but his green eyes were sincere. "Eve, I asked you to give me a chance yesterday morning because I could see how difficult it is for you to trust. Eve, it's your fear making you believe I'm lying to you. How can I prove I'm not?"

Eve gave him a sour smile and said, "You're feeding me another line. I know them all because, you see, I was married to a man just like you, except he was much better at it than you are, and I know how to trust people who deserve it, Dane. I trust Stanley, Gilbert and Jake just fine."

"That's because they don't ask for anything from you, Eve."

"You're quite right, Dane, they don't. What are you asking for?"

"Your love. But more than that, Eve, I want to give you my love."

His words stunned her. And for a moment, she wavered. Could he be telling her the truth? Was it possible Vanessa had lied to her?

"Eve, I know about the lodge and who really owns it. I know you're due for bankruptcy," Dane told her, his voice soothing, comforting. "I know pretty much everything, even that you and your cohorts kidnapped me."

"Frank told you?" she asked, knowing the answer and aching to believe Dane could be trusted.

"Yes."

"So buy in with Frank. It's a good deal," Eve said,

noticing Dane had moved close but unable to step back from him.

He shook his blond head slowly. "I'm not so sure it's a good deal with Frank or anyone else, but I'd like to help if I can." His eyes locked into hers and he brushed her cheek with his hand. "Trust me just a little, Eve," he pleaded.

She wanted to trust him. She truly did.

He pulled her into his arms and she let him. His mouth covered hers, expunging the anxiety of the past few days. She kissed him back, the touch of his lips beneath her own soothing past hurts, quelling the fear of losing him and the terror of loving him and hushing her troubled thoughts.

She felt his arms tighten around her and she raised her head, sighing with relief at being in his embrace. She never wanted him to leave her again. But he would leave her, she realized as he poured kisses along her throat. He would leave her tonight, or tomorrow after they'd made love, and he'd return to his Vanessa whom he'd betrayed, betraying Eve in the process. She'd permitted a man to ruin her life once before; she wasn't about to do so a second time, nor was she willing to ruin Vanessa's.

She pushed him away. "I don't believe you," she said flatly, "and I think it's time you left."

Dane's green eyes searched her face while his arms still held her. "You're afraid to believe me, Eve," he replied, his voice gentle, his face calm. "And with reason. You must have loved your husband deeply, but I'm not like him, and someday you'll come to see that."

He released her and went to the door, turning back briefly before he stepped outside. "I'd only need half as much love as you gave your husband because I'd know what to do with it ... I'd cherish it," he told her and then closed the door behind him.

* * *

No car passed to ease the isolation, no animal scampered across his path, no startled eyes peered into his lights. The road was black with only the universe above to light his way. The headlights on his truck cast gloomy shadows along the thick bush bordering the highway as he bounced along. It could be worse, he thought silently. It could be raining.

He didn't mind the solitary drive to Thompson. It freed his mind to think. He saw now that he'd been a fool to think Eve would fall into his arms simply because he'd come to her, offering to be her Sir Galahad. He grinned into the blackness at his own imagery. A knight in shining armor.

It seemed Eve had him turning up flowery prose at every turn. He didn't think it was so corny anymore, either. If it was part of what being in love did, it was fine by him. He wondered if all the torment Eve put him through was part of love as well. Something else to chew over with Nelson.

Dane lifted his thermos off the seat beside him, removed the lid and peered inside. Not a drop. He tossed it back. Who was he kidding? He wasn't going to be spilling his guts to Adsum. Nelson would think he was an idiot, and he'd be right.

The thing with Vanessa was a mystery. Dane had difficulty believing she'd told Eve she was his fiancée, but where else would Eve have gotten such an idea? He'd made it pretty clear to Vanessa he wasn't interested in marriage. In fact, he'd insisted she clear out all of her things from his apartment while he was gone.

It occurred to him that since Diane wouldn't have divulged any information whatsoever to Vanessa, Loewen must have called his apartment while Vanessa was there. He'd probably been trying to get a hold of him for days. Given how upset he was at having been kidnapped, he might have given Vanessa a little more information than was necessary. Or perhaps she'd pried more from him. Might he have been concerned about a possible relationship between Eve and Dane that would ultimately jeopardize his plans for the lodge?

What eluded Dane was Vanessa's motive in saying she was his fiancée. He could understand she might have been worried about him. They'd dated a couple of years, and he knew she'd been disappointed when they split up. He had assumed it was what she had wanted, since she'd told him she refused to see him anymore if he didn't marry her, that she needed to be free to find a man who could make a commitment. Maybe he'd misunderstood, although he couldn't see what there'd have been to misunderstand.

Women, who could figure them out? Dane asked himself, casting a thirsty glance at his empty thermos. It was going to be a long drive. The road became almost impassable for potholes. He shifted down a gear and hoped he'd been at least reasonably accurate in figuring out Eve. She was going to be a much harder conquest than he'd first guessed.

Back at the *Gas and Grill*, he hadn't argued with her further over Vanessa because he'd seen Eve was going to be slow in coming around to trust him. Pressing her further at this point would only have lost him more ground. However, her reluctance hadn't turned him away; it had simply been a detour. He knew how to wait. He'd once waited seven years for a contract to finalize. Eve was worth more than any contract he'd put together.

He shifted up again and drove on, not minding the silence or the long drive still ahead. It gave him plenty of time to think and formulate his plans.

* * *

Zipping up her jacket and closing the door behind her, Eve stepped into the black night, comforted that the long day had finally been consumed by darkness. Hearing the bad news late in the day from a despondent Gilbert and watching tears form in his eyes as they finally conceded defeat over the lodge had been as difficult to bear as the shocking revelations from Vanessa.

"What was their reason?" Eve had choked out as Stanley slumped into a chair, his head in his hands. "I thought it was a done deal."

"Still too risky," was all Gilbert could manage to say before turning away and shoving himself through the *Gas and Grill* door.

Eve had sat herself across from Stanley and taken his hand in hers. They had sat there for the longest time, neither saying a word, sifting through tortured thoughts, Eve thinking how it had seemed too good to be true right from the start. She'd later learned from Gilbert, when he returned to the restaurant after roaming aimlessly through the bush for hours, that it had ended up a five/four split, one Band Council member swaying to the opposing side at the last moment.

Eve sighed and allowed herself a heavy drink of the night sky above before marching towards the creek. It was her turn to roam. Funny how they all seemed to find peace in the woods. When they'd first been confronted with the reality of losing the lodge months back, Jake had packed a bag and disappeared for a week. It was Gilbert who had found him camping at the lake, a farewell of sorts.

She wished for the millionth time that she'd never dreamed up the idea for a lodge in the first place, but she'd started longing for something more when she was still with Bryce. It had begun as harmless escapism, a way to survive the never-ending evenings of staring blankly across the dinner table at the other equally bored and beautiful wives who'd been shut out of their husbands' business discussions and reduced to mere table decorations.

She supposed she'd cooked up the idea for the lodge because, of all the varied occupations and backgrounds from which Bryce's many clients and associates had come, it was the hoteliers to whom Eve had found herself drawn. Every aspect of the hospitality industry fascinated her, from property design and management to pleasing guests and motivating staff, and as her dreams began to take shape, she made a point of listening to the business discussions and gleaned whatever knowledge she could. She had even gone so far as to suggest to Bryce that the next time he listed the sale of a small hotel, they should consider purchasing it themselves.

Her proposal had severely annoyed him and he had quite bluntly told her to *stop daydreaming,* asking, *haven't I given you everything a woman could want?* to which she had sadly replied that she supposed he had.

Eve shivered. She should phone Vanessa and thank her. She'd almost been stupid enough to entrust her dreams to Dane. A tear surprised Eve and she angrily wiped it away.

She hoped Jake didn't feel he'd been stupid to entrust his land to her. She had shared with him her idea for a lodge at Lake of the Wolves after Mrs. Jake had died, partly to revive his spirits and partly to stimulate the dying community which she had come to love. Jake owned most of the land bordering the small lake and liked the idea, but instead of building it himself, he'd gifted the land to Eve and thrown his support behind her. The project had given them both a new focus. And the community hope.

Maybe she'd been a fool to accept Frank's money. But what had she stood to lose? The land was no use to anybody, undeveloped. Obviously, she didn't know as much about business as she'd thought; after spending so many years with Bryce, she should've automatically questioned Frank's integrity, but he was part of the community and he'd seemed so sincere at the time.

She raised her head towards the heavens. Was that the last of the hope for Jake's Corner? How could there be an end to it when the night sky stretched on forever? She couldn't help a twisted laugh. Maybe Bryce had been right. Maybe she was just a silly idiot with her head in the clouds.

One thing was for certain: she was still as naive and easily charmed as she had been back then.

Eve had almost dropped the phone when Vanessa had told her Dane was her fiancé, but she shouldn't have been surprised, she told herself now, tramping through the dark bush and patting the front pouch of her jacket to reassure herself that her flashlight was still safely tucked inside, even though the full moon amply illuminated her way. Hadn't she suspected all along that Dane wasn't all that he seemed?

Needing to know more, but careful not to arouse Vanessa's suspicions that Dane might have been flirting quite heavily with her, Eve had pumped Vanessa for information. She'd employed a friendly, chatty tactic which had only slightly softened the woman's strident demeanor.

"He's your fiancé?" Eve had asked, hoping she had recovered her poise enough to sound casual. "He's a handsome man. You must be very happy."

"Yes, the wedding is in May and I agree, he is indeed a handsome man, and rich also, as I'm sure you've noticed," Vanessa had sneered through the receiver. "Have you had much luck convincing him to rescue you from the backwoods and bring you to the big city?"

"Excuse me?"

"You know precisely what I'm inferring, dearie," Vanessa had snarled. "All you country girls attempt to escape your little hick-towns by sleeping with every man who passes through, but it's obvious you've been unsuccessful so far since you're still there, and I feel I must tell you that Dane Newson won't be your ticket out either. He leaves behind a woman like you everywhere he goes."

The woman's bitterness had convinced Eve of the truth, and a deep sympathy for Vanessa had welled within her. "You shouldn't marry him if he's already unfaithful," she had told her kindly. "He won't change for you later."

Vanessa's laugh had been shrill. "And leave him for someone like you? What's a little fling measured against all his money? Be honest, darling, it's his money you're after as well. Besides, he always comes back to me. And he always will."

"If all you can see is a man's money," Eve had retorted sharply, "then you two deserve each other. I'm sure you'll both be very miserable together."

She'd hung up the phone and then unplugged it. She didn't need to listen to that horrid woman again, and she certainly didn't wish to speak to Dane.

Eve continued her sombre amble along the creek to an obscure path. Veering onto it, she was soon immersed in blackness, the moonlight hindered by dense bush. She retrieved her flashlight from her pocket and lit up the path. Jake's hunting shack grew out of the shadows. She'd been walking for hours.

Eve expelled a weighted and melancholy sigh and tried not to think about the last time she'd been here with Dane. She pushed open the door, its hinges creaking raucously. Inside, she found a kerosene lamp, filled it with fuel and lit a match. Next she built a fire in the small cast-iron stove in the middle of the room and after untying a sleeping bag, crawled inside, using her jacket for a pillow.

She stared up at the moon through the solitary curtainless window. No one would bother her here. Stanley and Gilbert and Jake knew she often came here when she wanted to think. Dane had been right in that regard; they never made demands of her.

She sighed again. Wouldn't it have been wonderful if Dane had meant it when he'd said he loved her? Wouldn't it have been wonderful if he had been all those things he'd told her he was?

She rolled onto her back. There was no sense wishing for things that weren't possible. She might have lost her socks to Dane Newson, but she'd be darned if he took anything else from her.

She'd be all right in the morning, she told herself as she closed her eyes.

TWELVE

Eve opened a fresh box of chocolate bars and emptied them into the display case. Coffee, chocolate bars and gas. The three mainstays of the *Last Chance Gas & Grill.* Jake would have been broke long ago without them.

It had been just over three weeks since the Band Council's disappointing decision, but after the initial shock had worn off and a nervous Frank began evading questions as to his plans, Eve and her partners realized Newson Enterprises must have lost interest. They also suspected Frank was having difficulty finding another investor. And since he hadn't repossessed the lodge as he'd been threatening, they realized he likely didn't have the capital to finish building it either. If he repossessed, he wouldn't be able to squeeze any more money out of them.

The news had perked up all of Jake's Corner and renewed their hopes. And while Eve was thrilled for the reprieve and the burden it lifted, her feelings for Dane had not waned in the least and she was beginning to despair of ever getting over him. Despite every effort to control her feelings, each time a stranger appeared at the gas pumps, or a truck similar to Dane's pulled in, or someone ordered a chicken sandwich, she'd fall into the doldrums until she managed to argue her way out of it by reminding herself how narrowly she'd escaped becoming another one of his victims.

She'd managed to keep her suffering a secret until one morning when Andrew Cook unwittingly asked for "them fancy eggs with the sauce." She'd stared at him, chewing her trembling lower lip, and had torn off to the kitchen in a torrent of tears. After that incident, she noticed that the local folk carefully steered away from mentioning Eggs Benedict again, and in the most creative ways.

Someone would say, "I'll have eggs today, Eve," while their partner, spouse or otherwise would *tsk* and shake their head, saying, "But not them funny eggs you made when that Dang was here."

"Nobody wants those eggs," others would chime in consolingly, adding, "not that they weren't delicious, it's just that we don't want them again. Too highfalutin' for us simple folk."

Eve had to smile to herself, thinking about it again now and opening another box of chocolate bars. "Hey Eve!" Stanley called out to her from the restaurant where he and Gilbert were having lunch with Jake. "Look who's coming for a visit!"

Eve looked up from the chocolate bars to see Frank Loewen alighting from his car with a man whose attire and manner spoke of the big city. Toronto, again, Eve thought. Same trouble in the form of another person, she said to herself, closing the candy case and rising to her feet.

Judging by the tailored suit and expensive briefcase the man carried, it was quite possible Frank had snagged himself another investor.

"Afternoon, Eve," Frank greeted while his

companion gave her a polite nod. His dark hair was greying at the temples and his moustache was also peppered with grey, and an interesting streak of white ran through the front of his hair at the brow, causing Eve to suspect it had been there all of his life. "This here is Hartley Whitman of Meg-Mead National Inc., out of Toronto. Maybe you heard of them before?"

At least the guy wasn't a lawyer, Eve thought, extending her hand, saying *no she hadn't* and giving him the kind of smile she knew had blinded many a man. She could see Hartley Whitman's dark eyes appraise her quite frankly, like what they saw and then dismiss her entirely, as if she were no more than a nice piece of furniture.

Frank didn't bother to explain what Hartley Whitman's company did but instead ushered him into the restaurant where they helped themselves to coffee, sat down at a table and pulled out several ominous looking documents from their briefcases, spreading them over the entire surface.

Stanley and Gilbert remained glued to their own seats at their table across the aisle, drinking their coffee, pretending disinterest while Jake continued to be absorbed with his meal. Frank didn't bother to introduce them to Hartley Whitman.

Eve, having followed Frank and his companion, leaned against the door jamb for a minute and then asked, "Can I get you gentleman something else?"

"No, no thanks," Hartley Whitman said with a polite, slightly distracted shake of his head. "Coffee's fine for now."

His voice was crisp and polished. Eve folded her arms across her chest in disdain. Hmpf ... if he was hooked up with Frank Loewen, he was either a fool or a crook. She should know, having been fool enough to get involved with him herself.

"Explain to me again how you would cut a road from the lodge to here?" Hartley asked Frank, pointing outside to the intersection of Jake's Road and the highway.

Eve glanced over at Gilbert. They were going to build a road to the lodge? There'd be no need to fly in then, but it would seriously reduce the seclusion.

Frank caught Eve's eye, smirked, and then smugly began to reply, "Well, I thought since the bush has been cleared from this point here." He pointed to a spot on a map. "It would — "

"Never mind," Hartley cut in. "We wouldn't want a road there. We'd try to bypass Jake's Corner and intersect farther up where we could have our own gas station and restaurant; that way we could operate more independently and ensure every place our guests came into contact with would be first class. Moreover, since we'd own the land, there'd be fewer local district laws to contend with. Now, how qualified do you think these hunting guides are?"

Eve's mouth fell open. So did Stanley and Gilbert's. They were going to build a new gas station and restaurant? Jake might as well close his doors right now! He'd never be able to compete with a fancy new place. Besides, if this Meg-Mead National Inc. was a huge company, they would be able to purchase supplies at much lower prices. They'd easily undercut Jake and lure even his loyal customers away.

Jake had finished eating and was slurping his coffee, listening to Frank and Hartley along with

Stanley and Gilbert, but was seemingly unperturbed by what he heard.

"Well, they're pretty good," Frank replied, his confidence returning enough to sneer in the direction of the table beside him, "but they're not professionals."

"Precisely what I'm driving at," Hartley said before taking a swift sip from his own cup, setting it down carefully, away from the papers, and making a few notes with his gold pen. "We'd want to guarantee success for all our guests, be they fishers or hunters. That would require professionals. Which brings to me another point — lodge staff should be imported as well. Locals are convenient, but they won't have the degree of training we'd prefer. Service in an upscale operation like this has to be top-notch."

Eve was livid! How dare Frank Loewen and this insensitive stranger, who knew nothing about the people at Jake's Corner, suggest they couldn't provide competent labour or be capable of guiding hunters around their own territory. Besides, the cultural flavour that the local people would lend to the running of the lodge had been the very thing Eve had thought would make the lodge an attraction for foreign guests. These creeps didn't own her lodge yet!

She marched over to Hartley Whitman and leaned over his papers. "Has Frank mentioned by chance that he doesn't own this lodge just yet?" she asked sweetly. "It's a minor detail he sometimes neglects to tell prospective investors."

Hartley gave Eve a wide grin, his neatly groomed moustache spreading over his even white teeth.

Under different circumstances, she might have thought him handsome. "Yes, Ms. Barron, he did inform me of that, but since foreclosing on you people is a mere formality, I consider that information a minor detail also."

"Well, Mr. Whitman, the lodge doesn't belong to him yet, so until it does, I think you might be wise not to count your chickens before they're even eggs," Eve replied with a sideways smile as she borrowed Jake's twisted cliché.

"Ms. Barron," Hartley countered, his smile brutal, "are you telling me that you folks have found yourselves a hero willing to rescue you from your plight? Because, it would seem to me, from looking at Mr. Loewen's documentation, that's the only salvation you have left. However, since champions of lost causes are a rare species these days, I'd say I can quite comfortably proceed with my plans."

"Proceed away," Eve retorted, "but just remember, you don't own it yet, and we're not prepared to let it go until we've exhausted every resource available."

And with that she flounced back into the convenience store and feigned preoccupation with stocking candy shelves, intimating to Frank and his buddy that she wasn't the least bit worried over their plans to foreclose.

"Yeah, what she said!" Stanley declared in his dumb-guy accent, rising from his chair and exiting the restaurant.

"Me, too!" Gilbert added, following his partner out.

"Yep!" Jake muttered, scraping his chair against the floor and joining the exodus.

The three of them leaned over the counter and

winked at Eve. "That's telling them!" Stanley whispered.

"I guess our only remaining recourse is a miracle," she grinned up at him, despite her anger and sinking heart.

"A miracle ain't so impossible," Jake muttered, patting the counter top affectionately before shuffling to the door.

"No, but is it likely?" Gilbert asked, holding the door.

No, it wasn't likely, Eve answered silently, filling the empty chewing-gum shelf.

* * *

Dane pushed away the pieces of paper in front of him and leaning on an elbow, combed his hair with his hand. Diane had dropped off the last of her reports on his desk this morning. He reached over and flipped through them absently. Now that he understood precisely why Eve and her pals had lost the lodge, he was confronted with what, if anything, to do about it.

He casually wheeled his chair around, a panoramic view of his beloved Toronto and Lake Ontario spreading out before him through a wall of ceiling-to-floor windows. He wished Eve could know the Toronto he did. She always spoke of it with a disdain he surmised was rooted in her experiences with Bryce.

Sure Toronto had its share of crime and other problems that came with a city its size, but it was also vibrantly alive with ordinary folk who went to work, loved their families and cared about their neighbours. Jake's Corner didn't have a monopoly on those things.

However, Jake's Corner didn't have the sleepy clubs he liked or neighbourhoods of every possible ethnic nationality filling the air with their music and tantalizing culinary aromas. Nor could it boast venues for every conceivable activity and form of entertainment, of which professional sports and theater were just the beginning. In fact, as an entertainment centre, it ranked with the best, falling behind only London and New York. Some authorities would argue that it was the number one place to live in the world.

He had to agree. He'd been in major cities around the globe, and although all of them had the hustle and bustle of round-the-clock people and traffic, outstanding architecture, unique attractions and, yes, even smog, none had the same feel to its pulse that Toronto had. It was the heartbeat of Canada. And he was sure Eve could love it if she looked at it from a fresh perspective.

Dane shook his head woefully at his sentimentality and grinned out at the city. Eve had left her mark on him; he was a changed man. A blithering fool of a man who hadn't had a decent night's sleep since he'd left Jake's Corner because the instant he closed his eyes, wild brown eyes, a teasing smile and soft curves flashed before him, their images pursuing him relentlessly until dawn.

Concentrating on work, apart from anything involving Jake's Corner, was next to impossible; hanging out listening to jazz bored him, as did pretty much any social activity, and looking at another woman, even in passing, was out of the question. He invariably wound up comparing them to Eve.

The only time he was able to channel his attention

was in the weight room or on the racquetball courts, or roller-blading in High Park. Being patient wasn't as easy as he had thought it would be. He grinned to himself. If nothing else, Eve had ensured he would remain physically fit for quite some time.

He turned his chair back to his desk and checked his desk calendar. Nelson was due back in a couple of days. He circled a date a few days farther along the calendar. They had tickets to a hockey game.

He quashed, for the he-didn't-know-how-many-th time, the thought of flying out to Jake's Corner and instead punched in Angie's extension number on the telephone. That hockey game couldn't come too soon. He was going crazy.

"Yes, Mr. Newson?" his administrative assistant inquired upon answering his ring.

"Would you find me the number, please of ..." Dane thumbed through the papers, "Shepsky Real Estate in Thompson, Manitoba?"

"Sure thing. Right away," Angie replied.

"No more calls from Vanessa?" he asked. Vanessa had continued to call every couple of days since his return to Toronto, always with an offer to meet over lunch and reconcile their relationship.

"Not for three days now," Angie replied, sounding relieved that she didn't have to deal with her anymore.

Expelling a heavy sigh, Dane stood up and faced the windows, his hands deep in his pockets. Maybe having finally met with her had set things straight.

"Darling, I called that little hick-town because I was worried," she had pouted in a way he'd once found seductive. "When that strange man, Frank Loan or *something-or-other,* called your apartment, saying you were two days late and that he thought you might have had an accident, what was I to do? Thankfully, he had the wits to suggest calling that little rest stop to see if you had turned up there. I'd have been sick with worry otherwise."

"You said we were engaged. I was under the impression we were both quite clear on where things stood between us."

"I might have suggested something along those lines," Vanessa had replied with a smooth smile. "How else was I supposed to get them to take me seriously? You know yourself, it's nearly impossible to get information from a hotel about guests when you aren't a family member."

"A summer wedding?"

"Dane, really, you're making too much of this," Vanessa had continued in her sultry voice. "I was worried, that's all. What does it matter anyway? I can understand that you were stranded and they took you in, but those rustic folk can't possibly mean anything to you."

"Actually, Vanessa," Dane had said, wishing he didn't have to hurt her but there seemed no other way, "someone there does mean something to me. A lot, actually, and if it wasn't clear before, make no mistake about it now. It is over between us."

Vanessa's face had turned red with rage. "Don't come crying to me when you're bored with your little tramp. I won't take you back," she'd hissed.

Dane had watched her leave and had asked himself the same thing he was asking himself now: what had he ever seen in her?

* * *

Eve sat up and, wrapping her arms around her legs through the covers, hunched her knees to her chin. Despite the moon, her room was dark, but her mind was restless. To continue to strive for sleep was pointless.

She pulled the covers close about her and remained sitting on her bed. She knew what she should do; the question was, could she humble herself enough to actually carry it out?

If it were only herself who would be hurt by Meg-Mead National taking over the lodge, it wouldn't matter, but Hartley Whitman's plans to exclude the people from Jake's Corner from working at the lodge in any capacity, together with his intention to replace the *Gas and Grill* with his own version of a rest stop, spelled certain death for what little economic life Jake's Corner had left.

Moreover, it had been her and Stanley and Gilbert's intention to fly their guests to the lodge. The seclusion of Lake of the Wolves was to have been an advertising feature. Not to mention that a road might have disturbed the wildlife and destroyed the pristine quality of the surrounding forest. A plane had seemed the best compromise. They'd even put a large deposit down on one.

She sighed. She should have left things alone at Jake's Corner. Granted, it had been decaying long before she had come along, and the lodge had merely been an attempt to revive the community, but she couldn't help but feel that if Meg-Mead National took over, the people at Jake's Corner would be even worse off than before and she would be to blame.

Going to Toronto to try and talk Dane into buying the lodge made sense. Well, okay, so maybe it was more desperate than sensible, but what alternative was there besides begging Hartley Whitman to change his mind with regards to hiring local people? And after having met Hartley, she realized that if either of the two men were like Bryce, it was he. Despite being quite handsome, Hartley was a cold and brutal man. While Dane might be equally ruthless, selfish and devoid of conscience with regard to women, he possessed a certain warmth that gave rise to the smallest of hopes that — even if he'd been merely attempting damage control for having been caught in a lie — he still might actually honour his offer to help her out.

How much would she have to grovel? Eve asked herself. And would Dane expect something from her in return? Would he want her to sleep with him? Her shoulders stiffened rebelliously at the thought. He either bought the lodge or didn't. She'd beg on behalf of the people she dearly loved, but that was as far as she was willing to go.

She hoped.

It was dangerous to even contemplate going to see Dane. Her pulse was already racing at the mere thought of his green-eyed grin and deadly kisses and had her entertaining absurd ideas that perhaps Vanessa had been the one who had lied. Hadn't the woman practically admitted she was only interested in Dane's money? It was possible Vanessa had wanted to ensure that she kept Dane to herself. It was possible she had believed Vanessa instead of Dane because, as he had said, she was afraid not to. Wasn't it also possible that he really was all those wonderful things he'd told her he was outside Jake's hunting shack? What if Dane truly did love her?

The very thought warmed her through. He'd said

he'd only need half as much love as what she'd given Bryce.

Eve shook her head at her own silliness. Vanessa could not possibly have known that Dane had been trying to seduce her unless it was something he did on a regular basis. And the fact that he was involved with a woman who was in every way what Bryce had demanded she be sickened her. Dane was no different. He wanted a trophy on his arm and a playmate in his bed. Eve had merely been a way of passing time while he was waiting for his truck. Dane had probably long forgotten her and Jake's Corner and was likely unscrupulously chasing one new conquest after another while poor Vanessa sat at home, making out her wedding invitation list. She was eternally grateful she'd kept her wits about her enough to keep him out of her bed, and maybe she was a fool to think he would even consider doing her the very large favour of saving Jake's Corner. She could almost talk herself out of it if she weren't so desperate.

Through the thin walls, she could hear coyotes howling and despite her worries, smiled, recalling how the first time she'd heard them at Jake's Corner, she had thought they were wolves. Lake of the Wolves had been named inappropriately, Eve mused. It should have been Lake of the Coyotes, since there didn't seem to be too many of the former in the vicinity, while the coyotes seemed to be plentiful. Eve had only seen a wolf on two occasions, both times at a distance, and one had quite likely been a coyote since she still confused the two.

Eve tossed aside the covers and jumped out of bed, hastily throwing on her flannel housecoat against the chill of her room. She stepped into slippers and padded down the hall and stairs, exchanging her slippers for boots at the back door before pulling on her jacket and slipping outside.

She breathed the autumn night air deeply into her lungs and immediately her tortured thoughts vanished. She could always think better outside, especially at night.

THIRTEEN

Dane watched Nelson scale the steps two at a time, hot dog in hand, baseball cap on backwards and balancing his jacket over his arm.

"You can't judge the game by the score," Dane told Nelson absently, his eyes darting from the ice to the scoreboard as Nelson seated himself. "It's three to zip halfway through the first period, but we're outplaying them."

"I won't lose faith yet," Nelson promised. "Chicago's got a strong team this year, but our Leafs have never looked better." He bit into his hot dog before adding with his mouth full, "Thanks for warning me, by the way. In all of five seconds, she could have had me willing to crawl through mud and chew on rocks."

Dane chuckled. "I couldn't very well send in an unarmed man."

Nelson's laugh broke off as he sprang from his seat, flailing his hot dog about in frustration as he yelled, "Somebody get that ref a pair of glasses," the rest of the crowd bellowing with him.

He sat back down and said, almost in passing, as they concentrated on the hockey game, "I think she took the bait." Dane's only acknowledgment was in the form of a small smile and a slight nod of his head

as Nelson grinned. “But then you knew she would.”
A fight broke out on the ice between two players, temporarily diverting their attention. The fight was soon settled, the instigator exiled to the penalty box and the game resumed.
“So, do I finally get to be the best man?” Nelson asked, not taking his attention from the ice.
Dane arched an eyebrow, surprised by his friend’s question. “We broke up weeks ago. You knew that. Besides, Vanessa hates your guts. She’d never allow you to be best man.”
Nelson laughed. “Lots of people hate my guts.”
“That’s because I pay you to be miserable.”
The two men laughed.
“I wasn’t referring to Vanessa,” Nelson said a few minutes later.
“Eve?” Dane asked, his voice dry and forced. It wasn’t often he said her name out loud.
“Yes, Eve,” Nelson laughed. “Your days as a bachelor are numbered, buddy.”
“Since when did you become an expert?”
Nelson laughed again. “After the mission you just sent me on, you’re going to pretend you haven’t been knocked flat on your face?”
“It wasn’t like that,” Dane grumbled.
“Sure, buddy, I believe you, too,” Nelson chuckled and jumped from his seat as the Maple Leafs finally scored a goal.
“So how do you manage it? You and Anna,” Dane inquired offhandedly when the activity on the ice stopped for a television-commercial break. “I swear, you’re the only couple on the planet who’s still in love after ten years.”
Nelson cast a quick glance at Dane and then turned his attention back to the ice, pulling his cap from his head and releasing the wayward shock of white to

fall forward on his brow, a startling contrast to his dark hair. He twisted the peak of the cap in his hands for awhile and then said in an undertone without taking his eyes from the ice, "We work at it, Dane, because we both promised we would. The pay off is ten years later I still love her and she still loves me."

"It's that simple?"

Nelson chuckled softly and looked sideways at Dane. "No, it's not simple, but it's well worth it."

Dane smiled into the crowd. Hard work had never scared him.

The Leafs scored another goal and the arena went wild with joy, Dane and Nelson joining in the loud fracas.

"By the way, they're a bunch of kooks," Nelson said as they stood and cheered. "And I owe you payback for the name."

Dane laughed. "You needed to be as unlikeable as possible."

* * *

Eve untied the last knot and pulled the tarp off the little white car that had brought her to Jake's Corner four years ago. Bryce had refused to let her own a car and had been furious when, months before they separated, she had finally defied him by buying one. She had known she would need it if she was going to leave him. She seldom used it now, but Gilbert and Stanley always made sure it was in prime running condition for her anyway.

There was no need to be so quiet. She was the only one at the *Gas and Grill*, but nevertheless, she carefully opened the door, slipped inside and started the engine. She allowed it to warm only a few minutes before moving forward, lest someone happened along and asked where she was going. She almost laughed. Who would be around at three o'clock in the morning?

Ten minutes later she was bounding along the highway, wondering if her courage would last all the way to Toronto. If she could force herself onto a plane in Winnipeg, she supposed there'd be no turning back after that, unless, of course, Stanley and Gilbert managed to catch up with her before the plane left the ground. She hadn't told them or Jake of her plans. She knew they would have tried to stop her, but she'd left them a note by the coffee maker.

She settled back into her seat and mentally prepared herself for the long solitary drive to Winnipeg. What awaited her in Toronto she could only guess.

* * *

It was six o'clock in the morning when Dane hung up the telephone and bit back a grin. Oh what the hell, he thought, walking into the kitchen of his condominium to turn on the coffee maker. Live it up and let loose with a great big self-satisfied smile. He emerged a moment later, grinning like a kid in a toy store. Seating himself at his desk in the den, he allowed himself a tuneless whistle while he worked. She was on her way.

* * *

Eve retrieved her lone piece of luggage and surveyed the waiting queue of taxis and limousines, trying to decide whether to find a hotel first or simply head straight to Newson Enterprises. She supposed there really was no point in securing a room if she was going to wind up on the next available flight back to Winnipeg, which was where she'd find herself if Dane refused to see her or turfed her out onto the street after she'd pled her cause.

She approached a taxi, confronted by the memory of how Bryce used to whistle one down for her whenever he had to rush off in his limo. Pushing the image aside, she gave the driver her suitcase, climbed into the back seat and after giving him the address of Newson Enterprises, sat back and watched the city go by, amazed that Toronto was even more enormous than she remembered. Much of it had changed, but it was strangely comforting to see the CN Tower keeping its faithful watch over Canada's favoured metropolis.

Driving into a city the size of Winnipeg earlier in the day had been a shock to her system, but Winnipeg was a mere dot on the map in comparison to Toronto. She hadn't realized how isolated she'd been over the past few years. Eight lanes of frenzied traffic whipping along the Gardiner Expressway made her dizzy, and she had to struggle to remain calm. She didn't dare lean over the front seat to see how fast the taxi was going, but she knew Bryce's Porsche used to clock in at one-hundred-and-forty kilometres an hour.

She laughed, her father's bold assessment echoing from the past. "You'll only get to the traffic jam sooner," he'd commented with a smug snort when, during a visit, Bryce had taken him for a hair-raising spin through the city.

Eve gazed out the window again, almost in disbelief. Had she really lived in this? It was ten years ago when she'd first come to the city. At eighteen, she'd been barely an adult and far too vulnerable. Her life as a motherless child with a frequently absent father whose military career had consistently moved them across Canada and abroad should have provided her with the hardiness and experience necessary for survival anywhere, but it had merely left her rootless and yearning for a place to call home.

So when her father, ever an adventurer, had requested one final posting overseas before retirement, she had opted to stay behind and take a stab at independence, despite his apprehension that she might be too young. She had argued that she was practically on her own anyway since he was often away and her sister was off globetrotting with her new husband. He'd rolled his eyes heavenward when she'd looked at a map of Canada and pointed a finger at Toronto. However, she had made a concession by agreeing to stay just outside Toronto, in Oakville, with friends of his until she could find a job.

It began to rain, and as Eve watched the driver turn on his windshield wipers, she realized she'd neglected to bring an umbrella. Would her life have been different if she'd brought one to her first job interview, or would she have inevitably fallen victim to any man who had offered her a home?

For three long weeks, from her temporary home among strangers in Oakville, she'd mailed a multitude of résumés in response to newspaper ads, but there had been little call for a young woman with no skills or experience, unless one counted the ability to speak three languages and having lived in half a dozen countries. So, when an accounting firm had called to arrange an interview for a position as a receptionist, she had been nearly beside herself with excitement.

It hadn't been raining in Oakville that morning when she hopped onto the GO Train for the first time, thrilled about the possibility of working on Bay Street, amid Canada's financial mecca, and so she was mortified when the train rolled into Union Station, in downtown Toronto, amidst a pounding downpour.

Waiting in line to disembark, she tried not to panic as she realized that despite the instructions she'd committed to memory, she hadn't the vaguest idea where to go next. Nor had she expected the mayhem that greeted her as she stepped off the train. Hurried throngs of people, crammed together as one and streaming past, swept her up in their flow and pushed her along.

"If you get lost, just follow the crowd," her father's friend had told her.

Taking that advice literally, Eve followed the horde underground to the concourse, moving too rapidly past countless shops and restaurants to properly note any of the exit markings she'd been instructed to watch for. She made several attempts to ask for directions, but everyone was in a dreadful hurry, and it wasn't until five minutes past the appointed time for her interview that an older gentleman took a moment to inform her she was a fifteen-minute walk in the wrong direction.

Horrified, she bolted through the nearest exit, thinking it might still be possible to salvage the interview if she hailed a cab. Rushing into the street without thinking, she was immediately soaked to the skin as the sky doused her with every last drop of water in its possession.

Standing on the curbside, watching professionally dressed men and women clip past, beneath the shelter of umbrellas, their briefcases neatly in hand, she looked down at her own thin skirt and blouse clinging limply to her bones and burst into tears while water ran off her long hair and pasted it to her head. Her father had been right. She wasn't ready to strike out on her own, and she'd been a fool to attempt it. She couldn't even get to a simple job interview. Who would hire someone arriving late and looking like she'd nearly drowned along the way?

To this day, she didn't know how long she'd stood there on the street corner, missing her father terribly and too despondent to do anything but cry into the downpour and ponder her bleak future. She only knew that the rain had abruptly stopped, its hindered drops pattering above her.

"Are you lost, or do you always stand on street corners and sob into the rain?" a silken voice had asked smoothly from behind.

She'd turned to find a much older, but very handsome man holding his umbrella over her, exposing his own locks and obviously expensive suit to the elements.

Eve squeezed her eyes shut and forced the memory away. She didn't want to remember his consoling words, his caring eyes, or his kindness, but a piece of her heart grieved still for the love he'd shown at that moment and throughout their early days. But Bryce's love had been superficial, having gone no deeper than her body. "It was only because your wet clothes revealed all your secrets," he'd laughed with a sneer years later when she'd sadly asked where that love had gone. "Every man on the street that morning wanted a taste of you. I was the only one smart enough to take advantage of the opportunity to help you out."

"This is the place," the taxi driver announced,

startling Eve out of her gloomy thoughts as the cab pulled to a stop out front of a mammoth-sized building covered in gleaming copper and glass.

For a moment she considered asking him to take her back to the airport, but taking a deep breath, she climbed out, thanking him with a tip after he'd deposited her suitcase on the sidewalk beside her.

Eve gaped down the unfamiliar street, past the steady flow of traffic and the people teeming about, and then stared up to the top floors of the imposing building in front of her, wondering which one housed Dane's firm.

She glanced down at her wool suit. When she'd pulled it from the back of her closet at the *Gas and Grill*, it had looked rather chic to her eyes. It had cost a fortune — even for Bryce — but it was at least six years old. She fingered the lapels and wondered if the fashion was wide or narrow these days. Were skirts long or short? She hadn't even thought to notice, and to top it off, her suitcase, though also expensive, was noticeably out-of-date. She touched a hand to her hair; likely it was a sorry sight as well. She must look as out of place and inept as she had that first day so long ago when Bryce had swept her up.

Bewildered and on the verge of tears, she realized it had been ludicrous to think she'd be able to sail into Toronto, distanced from and unaffected by her past. She watched a limo roll by. Once upon a time, riding in one had been an everyday event. The closest she came to that these days was a bumpy ride in Jake's precious *Sweet-Pea*.

She smiled. Nothing could substitute for her wonderful, wizened, old chauffeur at Jake's Corner. Her smile deepened as she imagined what fun she would be having if Stanley and Gilbert were with her right now.

She laughed, discovering that she was no longer afraid of the myriad of emotions and memories shadowing her. They were only memories. Feelings. She'd long ago ceased being the little lost waif that Bryce had taken advantage of and tried so hard to control. In fact, all the pain she'd endured to reclaim her freedom was what gave her the strength to be the woman she was now. She should almost thank him.

She turned her face into the soft, warm breeze, finally feeling the release of Bryce's hold on her. Maybe, if there was time, she'd do a little sightseeing and get to know a different Toronto from the one Bryce had shown her. After all, Dane and a few million other people seemed to love it. Maybe she could love it, too.

She looked down at her clothes again and reminded herself why she'd come. So what if she was a country-bumpkin-come-begging?

She raised her chin, straightened her shoulders and pulling her luggage along behind her, proudly made the trek across the concrete. Pushing on the polished revolving doors, she smiled.

What did it matter that her shoes were practically antiques?

FOURTEEN

Dane was with the office manager when Eve stepped out of the elevator and glided regally down the hall past the glassed-in spaces, her luggage following behind like an adoring entourage. Every male head on the floor turned to take in long, silk-encased legs, a gorgeous figure a potato sack couldn't hide and that provocative smile he recalled so well.

No, she didn't have an appointment, he could see her informing the receptionist, *but, yes, she would be happy to wait.* She took a seat on the leather couch, crossed those incredible legs, picked up the latest copy of the financial news from the marble coffee table in front of her and began to read with interest, ignoring everyone around her.

She hadn't seen him watching from the manager's office, and Dane laughed softly to himself. That was the Eve he remembered — as spunky as ever. He returned to his own office and closed his door. It wouldn't hurt her to have to wait awhile.

* * *

Eve continued reading, determined not to glance at her wristwatch, although she suspected she'd been waiting for close to an hour.

"Ms. Barron?" a petite blonde inquired from the hallway behind the receptionist.

"Yes?" Eve replied, slowly looking up from the paper.

"Mr. Newson will see you now."

Eve stood up and leaving her suitcase by the couch, followed the woman all the way down the hall to the end where she opened a heavy oak door and announced, "Ms. Barron is here."

Eve stood in the open doorway, frozen by the panoramic view of downtown Toronto and Lake Ontario which the two walls of ceiling-to-floor windows exposed, her eyes sweeping over the opulence surrounding her, the art pieces gracing oak-paneled walls and the intimate conversation corner by one window. Her eyes dropped to the thick carpet beneath her shoes. Had she really lived like this once? It seemed like those affluent years with Bryce belonged to someone else.

"Eve," Dane said. "Please, come in."

She stepped inside and Dane's assistant closed the door behind her. He was standing beside his desk, and as much as she had tried to prepare herself, seeing him again was a shock.

She hadn't remembered his smile being quite so potent, or his dimples so deep, or his eyes so green. They warmed her now as he indicated the high-backed tapestry-covered wing chairs facing his desk. "Please have a seat."

She lowered herself into the nearest one and watched him round the desk to his own.

"Coffee?" he asked. "Or water maybe?"

She shook her head, staring at him in silent

evaluation and wanting desperately to believe the kindness in his face. She looked away. She should have never come.

"What can I do for you, Eve?"

She looked back at him. She had come, and so she might as well get on with what she'd come for. "It's not for myself, you understand, it's for them."

"Them?"

"Jake's Corner," Eve said. "Frank Loewen's found another company to take over the lodge, but this one will completely kill what little economy Jake's Corner has left."

Dane's expression was perfectly bland. "What exactly is it you think I can do?"

"Buy the lodge."

"How would that be any different from the new company?"

"They're planning to build their own road, and they say they won't hire locally."

"I see, and you think Newson Enterprises would be more considerate of the local economy?"

Eve nodded.

Dane appeared to think heavily for a long moment. "Your people did everything within your power to prevent me from buying the lodge, and now because a worse fate is about to befall Jake's Corner, I've suddenly become your salvation, and to top it off, you still don't trust me, Eve. What's in this deal for me? All I'd be getting is a partially built lodge which costs more than it's worth."

Eve lowered her eyes. Dane was right. Her sole hope for asking him to help was based on desperation and the things he'd said about himself at Jake's hunting shack. "I don't have anywhere else to go, Dane," she said, her words quiet.

"Tell me, Eve," Dane said, his voice silken and smooth, "exactly how desperate are you to save Jake's Corner?"

She raised her eyes. His face was still unreadable. "What do you mean?"

He gave her a slow grin. "I think I made it fairly clear when we were together how I felt about you. You'd be my sole reason for helping."

Eve jumped to her feet. "You're disgusting!" she shrieked. "I had you pegged the second I clapped eyes on you."

Dane threw back his head with a deep laugh. "You're far too willing to believe the worst about me, aren't you?"

"I'm sure I haven't thought the worst there is to know about you yet!" Eve retorted, furiously searching for her purse and not finding it. She must have left it in the reception area.

"Calm down, Eve," Dane said, still laughing. "I only wanted to know if you would be willing to stay in Toronto a few days while I put together a package to present to the Board of Directors. I was thinking we might be able to work out a presentation together. I do have controlling interest, but I still like to keep them happy, and to be honest, it's going to be a hard sell."

Eve stopped, having made it as far as the door. "Why would you do that?"

He rose from his chair and approached her. "Because, despite knowing how you feel about me, I still want to prove to you that I'm not the monster you think I am."

His green eyes swept over her face, and she could

see the last time he'd kissed her in his eyes. She remembered the taste of his lips, the feel of them on her throat and the desire to spend the night with him. She pushed away the memories and calmly held his gaze. Dane Newson was an accomplished seducer, and his effect on her hadn't lessened. "I'll stay as long as I have to, but only as long as we're working on the lodge. I'm grateful you want to help, Dane, but you need to understand, I'm not interested in anything other than a business relationship between us."

Dane smiled and opened the door for her. "I understand, perfectly, the relationship between us."

Eve stepped into the hallway, feeling like she'd made a bargain with the devil. Dane was not going to give up his seduction ploys so easily, and the way he had her blood racing, she knew she was going to be fighting herself as well. If she had any sense at all, she'd grab the first flight home and leave Jake's Corner to fate.

"Perhaps we can begin our discussion over dinner tonight," Dane suggested, escorting her along the hallway.

"No, I think I'd prefer we met during office hours and at your office." They were going to play by her rules as much as possible.

"I know some really great places to eat," Dane persisted.

"Toronto is full of really great places to eat, Dane. I'm sure I could find a few on my own."

They rounded the corner to the reception area and the first thing Eve noticed was that her suitcase had vanished along with her purse. The receptionist sat typing at her computer, pausing now and then to answer a call.

"Excuse me," Eve said, interrupting the young woman, "have you moved my suitcase?"

The receptionist looked up and appeared slightly confused by Eve's question. She glanced at Dane. "I'm sorry, but I didn't notice that you had left it here." She sounded more apologetic to her boss than Eve. "Are you saying it's gone?"

"Yes," Eve insisted. "I left it right there beside the couch. I think I left my purse there also."

"Oh dear!" the receptionist exclaimed. "So many people have come and gone. It's the close of the day, so the couriers have been buzzing in and out like flies, but I wouldn't think one of them took it. Is it possible you left it in the taxi?"

Eve shook her head, her heart sinking. "No, I'm sure I brought it with me, but my purse is gone as well." It wasn't much of a loss but it was all she had. She hadn't had a credit card in two years and she'd withdrawn the last of her savings to pay for this trip. She didn't even have a change of clothes. She had no choice now but to go back to Jake's Corner, sleeping at the airport while she waited for a flight. Tears filled her eyes. Fate seemed determined to beat her.

"Oh dear!" the receptionist claimed, passing over a box of tissue. "Please don't cry. I'm sorry, it must be my fault."

Tears poured down Eve's cheeks. She wasn't crying over her luggage; she was crying over everything. It was all becoming too much. Dane led her to the couch where she sobbed into a tissue.

"We'll replace your things, Eve," Dane told her soothingly, patting her hand. "If your luggage went missing in our office, then we're responsible."

"It's not your fault. I should have been more careful," Eve said between her sobs.

"I feel terrible," the receptionist said. "I should have been more observant; I guess I was just so busy, I didn't notice." She sounded worried her boss would chastise her.

"It's not your fault either," Dane told her. He turned back to Eve. "We'll put you up in a hotel and I'll open an expense account for you at a few clothing stores."

"I can't accept charity," Eve said, wiping her eyes and feeling a bit calmer.

"Nonsense," Dane insisted. "You opened your home, fed me, sheltered me and even fixed my truck. It's the least I can do. Besides, now we know we should install some sort of security camera out here. What if a client's briefcase went missing?"

"You weren't exactly staying with me by chance," Eve reminded Dane, blowing her nose.

Dane laughed softly and then gave her a green-eyed grin. "Maybe you're not here by chance either."

Eve's mouth dropped and her eyes widened in shock. Dane had kidnapped her?

He threw his head back with a laugh. "There you go again, believing the worst!"

FIFTEEN

Eve tossed her key onto the bed and surveyed the room. It was modestly decorated in a warm dark floral with an antique desk and wardrobe against one wall to complement the beds and armchair. A television, which she knew she would never watch, sat in one corner. Dane had booked her into the Royal York Hotel. It was close to his office, so she could have walked to it, but he'd insisted on calling a limousine.

She flopped onto the second bed and gazed through the sheer curtains. The view wasn't so special from her room, but she liked the hotel. It was elegant without being ostentatious and her room was cozy.

What she wasn't so comfortable with was being so completely dependant upon Dane. He'd arranged for her to make purchases in a few shops in the hotel, and she was also welcome to dine in any of the restaurants, but she had no cash. Anywhere else she went had to be within walking distance. She couldn't even take a taxi back to the airport. She was virtually a prisoner in the hotel. She wondered if Dane had felt as confined at Jake's Corner as she did now. What rotten luck to have her things stolen. Only a country bumpkin would have left luggage unattended the way she had.

She lay back and a little thought niggled its way into her mind. Was it possible her lost luggage wasn't a coincidence? She sat up, annoyed with herself. Dane was right. She was far too ready to see the worst. She rolled onto her side and spied the telephone. Somebody in Jake's Corner might be able to send her money. She really hated being dependant on Dane.

Eve dialed the number to the *Gas and Grill* and waited while it rang several times. No one answered. Next, she tried Stanley and Gilbert's garage with the same result. She continued dialing numbers until she'd exhausted her memory. No answer at Andrew Cook's, the Epps', or anyone's. She sighed. It was strange that no one answered their telephone.

A panic began to wash over her. She really was stranded. The more she thought about it, the more she needed to leave. She just couldn't stay here, dependant on Dane's whim. She had to escape somehow.

Eve told herself to calm down. She was overreacting. Maybe this was the feeling she heard people talk about when they came down from the North. There were too many people and too many things happening all at once.

She relaxed for a moment but then remembered she still had her plane ticket. All she had to do was get to the airport. If she explained her plight to someone, she might be able to beg enough money for cab fare.

She dug out the telephone book and called the airline.

"I'd like to book my return flight please," she said when, after responding to a number of automated questions, someone finally answered.

"I'm sorry, but you already took a flight back to Winnipeg," the ticket agent told her.

"How could I have possibly taken that flight if I'm still here?" Eve demanded.

"I'm sorry, ma'am, but I'm just telling you what the computer says."

"It's impossible," Eve shrieked. "What time did I leave?"

The man was silent for a moment. "I'm sorry, ma'am, but I can't tell you when or even if an Eve Barron was on any of our flights. We don't give out that information."

"I'm Eve Barron!" Eve told him. "Someone must have sold my ticket. My purse was stolen today!"

"Do you have identification to prove who you are?"

"No, of course, I don't! How could I?" Eve screeched.

"Well, ma'am, I don't know what to suggest. Have you called the police?"

"No," Eve replied dejectedly, hanging up the receiver.

She stared at the wall for a moment, trying to decide what to do next. Maybe she *should* call the police, but what would that accomplish? Incidents like this were an everyday occurrence in any city, and it wouldn't get her ticket back. Now, unless she could eventually get in touch with someone in Jake's Corner, she'd even be forced to beg airfare from Dane. Her sister was crawling through some jungle somewhere, filming wildlife with her husband, and her retired father was off globetrotting as well.

The little thought niggled her again. Maybe this

whole thing was an elaborate plot by Dane to pay her back for what they'd done to him in Jake's Corner.

She sat up. She was being ridiculous. She was thinking the worst again. She was suffering from culture shock. Dane was right. She was so willing to think the worst.

She asked herself again the question she'd been asking over and over since he'd left Jake's Corner. What if she had misjudged him? Well, then she'd thrown love away with both hands.

There was a knock on her door. She opened it and was greeted with a huge, beautifully wrapped basket containing every toiletry she could have imagined needing, from shampoo to expensive perfume, along with things she didn't need like a small bouquet of flowers, chocolates and mineral water. The note read: *Compliments of Newson Enterprises.*

Eve tried not to be disappointed Dane hadn't signed it and written something personal. If she had misjudged him, would he be willing to forgive her? Wasn't he still willing to help her even though she'd held onto her mistrust of him? Maybe he truly did love her.

Eve untied the large pink bow at the top and pulled down the cellophane. He might not have signed the card, or selected the items, but that he'd thought to send it made her feel his presence just the same. She fingered the sprig of autumn flowers — asters — and placed the vase on her desk.

She wouldn't trust him fully, but what harm would there be in giving him the small chance he'd asked for?

* * *

Dane accepted the bag from the clerk and

pocketed his credit card. He hoped he'd gotten the right size. He sauntered out of the store, whistling, a grin playing around his mouth. Revenge was so sweet.

* * *

Eve spread the clothes she'd bought on the bed and smiled at her choices. It turned out her expense account had been at a very chic boutique attached to a wing of the hotel lobby, so making frugal choices had been difficult; apart from necessary undergarments, she'd selected only one article of clothing — a black dress. She had her suit, the hotel provided bathrobes, and she could sleep in the nude. She wanted to owe Dane as little as possible. If she ever managed to earn a living again, she'd find a way to repay him, a dollar at a time if she had to, but the dress had been a weakness.

From the instant she'd spied it on the rack, she knew she had to buy it, not for herself, but for Dane because if he ever asked her out for dinner again, she'd accept and she wanted to be wearing that dress. She lifted it off the bed and held it up against herself in front of the mirror. She wanted to knock him off his feet.

A knock sounded at her door. She smiled. Maybe more flowers? Tossing the dress aside, she opened it. Dane, dressed in roller-gear, was standing on the other side, swinging several large shopping bags. He gave her a wide, dazzling grin.

"Strap on your knee pads," he said, "and I'll take you on one of my dates."

Eve accepted the bags, laughing when she saw a boxed pair of roller blades in one bag; helmet, gloves, elbow and knee pads in another, and tights and a baggy sweatshirt in the last one. "Revenge for the dirt bikes?"

"Are you game?"

* * *

She'd taken to the roller blades instantly, falling on her rear only twice. Holding hands, they had woven throughout downtown Toronto for a couple of hours while the nightlife came alive.

"Hungry yet?" he asked when they stopped for a rest.

She nodded, stooping over to catch her breath. "I think you're trying to kill me."

"I've got all sorts of wicked schemes in store for you," Dane laughed. "What would you like to eat?"

She shook her head, still breathless. "We can't go in anywhere in roller blades, and I'm too tired to skate back to the hotel. You're going to have to throw me onto a streetcar."

"I've got the perfect solution ... my condominium is right above you."

Eve stood up sharply and stared above her. She gave him a hard look. "I'm not going into your condominium with you."

Dane gave a soft laugh; she was so predictable to him now. How had he not been able to understand her before? "There you go again, assuming the worst. I've got all the reports we need for your lodge spread out all over my office. I thought we could order in and do some work."

She dug at the sidewalk with a skate, her hands on her hips through the bulk of her sweatshirt. She gave him a sideways, questioning stare. "We're going to work?"

He nodded.

She shrugged. "Okay."

Dane pressed the security code for the building door and grinned inwardly; he might have read her wrong, but he thought she might actually have looked disappointed.

"So, what'll it be, Eve?" he asked once inside, removing his roller blades. "There's a great little Italian place around the corner that makes the most wonderful shrimp linguine."

Eve dropped her roller blades to the floor. "Pizza! Oh, Dane, I haven't had a piece of pizza for —" She counted her fingers. "Four years — no, five. Wait. I bet it's been ten. Bryce never let me order pizza unless it had goat cheese on it."

Dane laughed. "Pizza? I offer you divine cuisine and you want pizza with — let me guess — pepperoni?"

"Yes!" she cried. "And lots of mushrooms."

Who'd have thought so little would make her so happy? While she wandered through the apartment, he dialed the little Italian place. She may as well have the best pizza. Through the corner of his eye he watched her roam about the living room, touching pieces of art she found interesting, lifting books and CD's from the shelves. What else had Bryce withheld from her, besides her happiness? he wondered grimly. The man had been a fool. She was a priceless treasure and all she required was love.

When she'd concluded her evaluation, she seated herself in the armchair by the window and sipped on the beer he'd poured for her. He grinned. She had placed herself as far away from the sofa as possible. He watched her stare out over the city for a few minutes and then rise and open the door to the balcony. She was so strangely quiet, almost shy, or maybe she was merely pensive. She must have a truckload of memories haunting her. He wanted to erase them all.

He followed her out to the balcony's edge. She didn't speak or even acknowledge his presence.

"Eve," he said, almost whispering.

She turned her head, fixing her dark eyes upon him. He wanted to kiss her so badly it made his heart ache. He'd promised himself he wouldn't, but unable to stop, his hands found her waist. She stared up at him the way he imagined she had once stared up at Gilbert or Bryce. She loved him. He no longer doubted it.

She abruptly turned back to face the city so that he could no longer read her eyes.

"So tell me about your plans for the lodge," she said lightly, and he knew tonight would not be the night for confessions of love or anything else.

"Come and look," he said, releasing her.

He sensed her relief as he led her into his office to begin the process of mapping out a plan to present to the Board of Directors. He showed her the original file he'd taken to Jake's Corner and the ideas he'd developed since.

The pizza arrived, and they ate while discussing what steps they needed to take before making a presentation. Eve was obviously tired, likely from both the roller-blading and the long stressful day she'd endured, and so her interest waned early. After awhile he saw that she'd stop listening to him altogether and was staring at him with a look of wonder. He ceased talking and smiled. Things were beginning to go his way.

He could see that now she would let him ... want him ... to kiss her. Maybe she'd want much more than a kiss but he wasn't leaving anything to chance. He'd almost blown it on the balcony. He knew perfectly well where even one small kiss would take them. There were still too many secrets between them. He didn't want to risk losing her, and he would if she had even one small regret.

She must have seen that he wouldn't kiss her because she turned her attention back to the notes she'd been taking and a moment later looked back up at him, her eyes dark as night. "Dane, I'm very tired. Would you take me to my hotel now?"

"It's late, why don't you stay here?"

She seemed to consider this for a moment, weighing in her mind whether or not she could trust him. It pleased him that she hadn't immediately jumped on him and accused him of attempting to seduce her. "Where would I sleep?" she asked.

"I have a guest room."

She thought for another moment. "Okay," she said finally, her voice burdened by fatigue, yawning deeply as he led her to her room.

Apart from the bathrobe and a few generic toiletries, he kept the guest room empty. He wondered if Eve would notice his condominium was free of anything which could even remotely be considered as belonging to a female.

Vanessa had cleaned out most of her things while he had been away, but she'd left a few items behind, which she seemed to remember from time to time, and often showed up unannounced to collect them.

These incessant visits had come to irritate Dane, and he had impatiently packed up everything he could think of which might possibly belong to her, including things he was fairly certain didn't, and had sent them over via courier a few days ago.

He knew he wouldn't sleep well with Eve down the hall, so leaving her, he had decided he may as well work. He was in the kitchen, putting on a pot of coffee, when she paused in the doorway, dressed in the terry bathrobe which was several sizes too large for her.

"Dane, was I wrong about Vanessa?" she asked, sounding frightened of his answer.

Dane stopped grinding coffee beans and smiled tenderly into those dark eyes. "Yes, Eve, you were."

She nodded, and after standing silently for a few minutes, lost in thought, wished him goodnight before gliding down the hall towards her room.

Dane went back to grinding beans. Another man might have gone after her, swept her into his arms and carried her off to his bed, but Dane wanted Eve *for keeps,* as the saying went, and he wasn't about to trade away all of his tomorrows for one *tonight*.

SIXTEEN

Eve yawned deeply and stretched. She hadn't slept so well in months. Laying against the pillows, she smiled up at the ceiling; there weren't any cracks or stains to occupy her. However, there was one very beautiful stained-glass light fixture. She counted the different coloured panes and then, losing count, had to start over. All in all, there were eleven different shades of blue.

She stretched again and rolled over to stare out her window at Lake Ontario. Dane had a beautiful view from his apartment. She wondered if he was still sleeping or if he'd gone off to work. Despite dying to see him, she hoped she had the place to herself. She needed some time to sort through her tumbling thoughts.

She couldn't precisely say when she'd realized Dane was the man of honor he claimed to be, but it must have been somewhere between working together in his office and his invitation to spend the night.

No, that wasn't it at all, Eve corrected herself, tossing aside the covers and jumping out of bed. It was when she realized that he'd never stopped thinking about the lodge. A man didn't come up with all his ideas in the space of a few hours; they were too methodically planned, and if he'd been thinking about the lodge, he'd been thinking about her.

He only needed half as much love as she'd given Bryce. Eve remembered those words with elation because it meant he'd be loving her in return. Why hadn't she seen the truth before? She marvelled at the incredible stroke of luck which had brought them together again. Would he have come back to Jake's Corner eventually? How would he have convinced her to trust him if he had? She didn't think his buying the lodge would have done it since it had been only her desperation that had forced her to accept his help in the first place.

She ran the shower in the guest bathroom and stepping inside, decided it had been the culmination of many things that had led her to discover the true man Dane was. It had been the basket, the roller-blading and that he hadn't been angry when he'd learned they'd kidnapped him. It had been everything about him that she'd been too stubborn to see.

She towelled dry, wrapped herself in Dane's bathrobe and padded barefoot down the hall. His bedroom was empty and so was the living room, but in the kitchen a note and an envelope waited for her on the table.

"*Hope you slept well, I didn't want to wake you. Please accept the money I've left you. I don't want you to feel stranded. You can book a flight home if you like and charge it to my account, but I'd prefer if you met me tonight for dinner. There are some things I need to tell you. Love, Dane*"

The bottom of the note contained the name and address of a restaurant and a time. Eve opened the envelope. It contained several large bills. She closed it up. She wouldn't take his money. She turned on the coffee he'd prepared and sat at the table, rereading the note while the coffee dripped.

Wasn't that just like him to want to ensure she was comfortable? How many men did she know, besides Stanley and Gilbert, who would let her stay in their apartment without trying to sleep with her? A smile played about her mouth. She'd just compared Dane to her two most favourite men in the world next to Jake and her father.

She fanned her face with the note and allowed the smile full reign. She'd go to that restaurant to meet Dane.

She stood up to pour herself a coffee when the doorbell rang impatiently. Cup in hand, she wandered down the hall, listening as it continued to ring, and then looked on the video screen to see a tall and slender, impeccably dressed, dark-haired woman with her back to the camera.

"Yes?" Eve asked, pressing the intercom.

"Mrs. Smithwood, let me in," the woman commanded.

Mrs. Smithwood must be the housekeeper. But who was this woman who was on such familiar terms with her that she could demand to be admitted to Dane's condominium?

"I'm sorry, but I'm not Mrs. Smithwood," Eve said into the intercom.

The woman whirled around and peered into the camera as if she could see who was speaking to her; then she raised an eyebrow. "Another overnight guest, are we? Well listen, darling, I'm Dane Newson's fiancée and if you aren't out of that apartment in ten seconds, I am going to make you very sorry."

Eve's heart sank to the bottom of her stomach. Dane had been lying to her. This woman was obviously Vanessa. How could she have been such a fool as to believe anything he said at all? Tears filled her eyes. And to think she'd been about to meet him tonight and give him the chance he'd begged her for! Thank goodness she'd been spared that humiliation. She ought to thank Vanessa for showing up like this.

"Hurry up and get out and buzz me up. If we're lucky we'll miss each other on the elevators," Vanessa snarled into the camera.

Eve looked at the unhappy woman through her tears. How could Dane love a woman like her? But then who wouldn't be miserable with a cheating fiancé to contend with?

She was about to buzz Vanessa into the building when she heard Dane's voice whispering through her mind, *You're always so willing to believe the worst.* She looked at Vanessa again. Though beautiful, her features were harsh — an outward expression of the inner person. Dane wouldn't love Vanessa. This woman was the liar, not him.

She pressed the intercom. "Vanessa, if you're Dane's fiancée, why don't you have a key?"

Vanessa's mouth fell open and she screeched, "Let me in, you little tramp. You're the hillbilly from that dump he got stranded in last month, aren't you? He told me all about it. You might have convinced him to bring you to Toronto, but you'll be on your way back the moment he gets bored."

Eve didn't bother to listen any longer. She smiled deeply. She wasn't threatened.

The doorbell began ringing again, but Eve ignored

it until it eventually stopped. She returned to her room. She'd take enough of Dane's money to pay for her taxi to her hotel and to the restaurant. She was so excited about the coming evening that she wasn't sure she'd be able to wait. She laughed out loud. She was free. Finally. Free of Bryce, free of mistrust, but most important, she was free to love.

Free to love Dane? Yes! her heart sang. She gazed out her window and wondered what he was doing at this precise moment. Would he, in some incomprehensible way, be able to sense her release while he sat working at his desk? She stared at the glaring rays of morning sun beaming into the room. Tonight was such a long way away.

She shrugged herself into last night's clothes, wishing she could tell him now. She paused, a smile forming on her lips. She would tell him now.

* * *

Dane again resisted the urge to call the condominium and instead gazed unseeingly out over Lake Ontario, envisioning Eve still slumbering as peacefully as when he'd looked in on her before leaving for work, needing to see for himself that she was still there and that last night hadn't been a dream.

He hoped she wouldn't be too proud to make use of the money he'd left her, but he prayed she wouldn't use it for a ticket home. He grinned in the direction of a few boats sailing across the horizon. If she did, he'd just have to find an excuse to follow her.

And he'd enlist Jake's help again if he had to. His grin widened. Much like begging a father for his daughter's hand in marriage, Dane had confessed his love for Eve to Jake. The old coot had taken it better than he'd expected and didn't seem all that surprised when Dane told him he was certain that Eve loved him in return but was throwing a lifetime of happiness away because she couldn't see past Bryce. Jake had grumbled his support of Dane's plans, promising to let him know when Eve was on her way and to come to his defence if the whole thing backfired.

He was confident it wouldn't, but Dane was prepared for the worst, since there was no sure-fire way of knowing ahead of time how she might react to his telling her everything tonight.

"Hey there!" Nelson announced with a quick double-rap on the open door before passing through and closing it behind him. He dropped a stack of files on Dane's desk. "This should just about cover it all."

* * *

Eve studied her reflection in the mirrored elevator wall, not caring that the other riders were watching as she did. She wasn't here to see any of them.

She'd had her hair trimmed and her make-up done at the hotel salon, laughing inwardly at the time because she'd run in and allowed the first available hairdresser access to her neglected locks. There had once been a time when no one but *James* was permitted to touch her hair, showing up at her luxuriant home whenever Bryce had decided that her long tresses needed the stylist's magic touch.

She touched her hair with a hand. It wasn't a whole lot different, just cleaned up and a little more current. Would Dane like it? She held her hands out in front of her and inspected her manicured nails. It was odd to see them painted again after so long. She hoped it wasn't too much. The dress, the make-up, the hair, but especially the dress ... okay, it was definitely overkill at ten-thirty in the morning, but she wanted to knock Dane off his feet and make him forget she had ever doubted him.

The elevator slowed and came to a halt. With one final glance, she waited for the doors to open, then stepping into the hallway, made her way towards the doors of Newson Enterprises.

SEVENTEEN

Dane passed Nelson the file he'd been perusing and leaned back in his chair. They'd been reviewing documents all morning, building an irrefutable case and plugging anticipated loopholes before they took any action.

He had to give Frank credit for imagination. And patience. He could have simply invested in the lodge and earned a healthy return down the road. Or for the paltry sum of five-hundred-thousand dollars, an amount he'd amassed after liquidating most of his assets, he could, instead, essentially rob Eve of a prime piece of land worth twice as much but falsely appraised at half its true value, scoop up a half-built lodge in the process and, apart from securing an investor to finance the remaining construction and operating capital, end up pretty much the sole owner of a potentially profitable venture.

The bogus environmental complaint was an inventive attempt to impede the construction of the lodge and thus deplete the financial resources of Eve and her pals, but Frank had underestimated their ability to make their loan payments long after they'd run out of the cash he'd lent them. Frank was now out of cash himself, which left him in a very weak bargaining position with potential investors. And with little hope of ever landing a buyer for his once flourishing but now near bankrupt Foster Rapids Tavern, he'd become desperate enough to put his house on the market last week.

Upon meeting Frank, Dane had instantly recognized a con man, but had he known earlier the full extent of Frank's corruption, he'd have informed Eve of the truth and never sent Nelson to Jake's Corner.

He stared past Nelson's head and argued with himself that he'd done the right thing regardless. She might not have believed him anyway, and he might not have been able to rescue her if Frank had managed to find himself a real Meg-Mead. There were plenty of them out there. At least by sidetracking him with a phony offer from Meg-Mead, he'd gotten Frank out of the way until he could figure out what was really going on. And baiting Frank hadn't taken more than an offhand remark that he was glad he'd been approached first instead of Meg-Mead National, a competitor which often outbid him.

"Should someone inform the police?" Nelson asked, closing the file and setting it on the desk.

Dane shook his head. "No, I think Frank will be quite co-operative in forgiving the loan and any claims he has to the land when he weighs it against spending time behind bars. As for his cousin, I'm sure he can make restitution for having falsified the land's value on the appraisal."

"Oh, you mean, something in the form of a large cash donation from Shepsky Real Estate to the hamlet of Jake's Corner for the construction of say, a town hall?"

"It's the least he can do. But I was thinking he might, instead, like to invest in the lodge, forfeiting any dividends, of course."

Nelson grinned. "It seems to me Frank did Eve and company a favour. They're going to end up in a better position than if the banks had simply lent them money in the first place. She won't need you at all."

Dane couldn't hold back a triumphant smile. "That puts me in the best possible position. She hates having to depend on anyone."

Nelson laughed outright. "Suddenly you're an expert on women?"

"Just one," Dane replied, his smile widening as he rose from his chair to follow Nelson to the door.

* * *

Eve flipped through another magazine and tossed it onto the pile beside her. Surely the receptionist should have returned by now. She'd been surprised to find her desk deserted but figured maybe the woman had slipped away to do a little photocopying or fetch office supplies. She glanced at her watch again. Eleven-fifteen was an odd time for a coffee break, but what else could explain her prolonged absence?

She vacated her chair and leaned over the desk. The switchboard continued to light up with calls, but perhaps they were being forwarded to another desk or an automated answering system. What did she know about office procedures anyway?

Eve stepped beyond the reception area and peered into the long hallway that led to Dane's office. Perhaps she would just go see if his door was open. No matter, if he happened to be in a meeting; she'd just wait a little longer. The receptionist had to return at some point.

"May I help you?" a handsome young man inquired, discovering her as he emerged from a nearby office.

"Is Mr. Newson busy?"

"I believe he's with the vice-president right now, but the receptionist should be back shortly. She can probably give you a good idea of how much longer they'll be."

* * *

"So I take it my rapid climb up the Meg-Mead corporate ladder is at a standstill?" Nelson quipped as he returned to Dane's desk to retrieve his forgotten suit jacket.

"Not unless you can convince my mother to step down as head of her little laundromat empire," Dane replied with renewed mirth, imagining the look on Frank's face should he ever meet his mother, Megan Mead-Newson.

Opening the door, he stepped into the hall and forgot everything he'd ever known. Conversing with an obviously entranced male employee, Eve stood at the end of the corridor, in high heels and a long-sleeved black dress, off-the-shoulder, skin tight and extremely short, a black sweater draped casually over one shoulder and no purse.

He wanted her.

He'd wanted her every breathing moment since she'd casually bounced down the steps of the *Gas and Grill* towards his truck and tossed a provocative little grin his way. He wanted her body, her thoughts ... her love, her soul. He wanted it all ... right down to kids and the dilapidated *Last Chance* if that's what she came with.

As if sensing him, she turned with a smile that knocked him dead, but it vanished as her eyes darted beyond him and then back again, her face turning white with shock.

Dane turned to look beside him and remembered Nelson.

Eve's mouth dropped open. "Hartley Whitman is your vice-president?" she screeched.

"Eve," Dane began calmly, "it's not as bad as it looks." At that, the male employee ducked into the nearest office, and Nelson followed suit.

Her breath was a strangled gasp. "It looks pretty bloody bad!" She tossed her sweater angrily at him, but it sailed impotently to the floor in front of her. She looked around impatiently and then kicking off a shoe, picked it up and threw it at him with a mighty force. He had to swerve; she was a good shot. She kicked off the other shoe, and then turned and fled, reappearing only long enough to fling the other shoe at him before disappearing again.

Dane almost laughed. She was mad as hell, but it could have been worse.

* * *

Eve pressed the elevator button furiously, then streaked to the stairs. She'd fly down all fifty-five flights if she had to in order to escape that scum-sucking snake like the one she'd been so stupid as to marry. Now there were two men in the world she never wanted to see again.

She stopped on the thirtieth floor to catch her breath and had an abrupt change of mind. Why was she the one running away? She had fled Toronto once without so much as a backward glance and without having unleashed her fury on Bryce. Dane wasn't about to get off so easy.

She pivoted swiftly and began stomping back up

the stairs, suddenly missing her shoes and blaming Dane for it and not finding her breath returning. She heard a door open some ways up and stopped to listen.

"Eve," Dane called out. She heard his descending steps. "Let me explain. I know it was a rotten thing to do." The steps stopped as though he, too, were listening.

"What's there to explain?" she snarled, surprised at how good it felt. With renewed anger and determination, she mounted another flight but found she lacked the energy to go much farther. She hadn't realized she was so out of condition. "It's all pretty obvious ..." she panted, "... to me. You're nothing but a lying, cheating ... uhm ...cheating ... liar!"

"I get the message," Dane called down, sounding amused as well as closer. She hadn't heard his continued descent.

Eve tried another flight of stairs, determined he wouldn't escape the full measure of her wrath. "You took my luggage, didn't you?" She paused for a breath and pressed on upward. "Was it payback for kidnapping you?"

She heard a short laugh and was enraged, but the anger only seemed to slow her down. She managed a few more steps and then summoned enough energy to call up to him, "Do you mind coming down here?"

His loud laughter rippled throughout the stairwell. "Are you out of shoes? I'm unarmed."

"This is hardly amusing, Dane," Eve panted and then giving up climbing altogether, sat down on a landing and waited.

"I agree." His footsteps didn't quite drown out his chuckles. "Your aim's quite accurate." A moment later he was sitting down beside her. "I'm all ears," he said with a slow grin.

"You tricked me," she accused, disappointed that her shortage of breath kept her from barking the words at him as she'd intended, desperately striving to keep her brows sternly furrowed together with him so close and watching her with an unwavering gaze.

"Ditto," Dane replied, not sounding the least bit angry and reaching for her hand.

"You lied to me," she continued, not pulling away and not wanting to, fresh out of accusations and breathless now from his touch, remembering the way he'd kissed her hands at Jake's hunting shack and how his lips on her fingers had lit a fire inside her.

"Ditto again," he repeated, his eyes caressing her face.

She asked herself, what had he done to her that she hadn't done to him first? "I suppose we're even then, are we?" she whispered, unable to draw her eyes away.

"Not by a long shot," he murmured, wrapping her in his arms and lowering his mouth to hers.

Eve surrendered to his kiss, the last of her anger vanishing with the wondrous discovery that it had merely been anger at having been beaten at her own game and nothing more. And nothing like the gut-wrenching anguish that had knifed through her with each of Bryce's betrayals. It had been anger, pure and simple, because she trusted Dane. And deep in her heart, she knew he was worthy of it.

Dane's lips strayed across her cheek before sinking into her hair. He kissed her ear. "Are you ready to trust me, Eve?" It wasn't really a question.

She pulled away, her breath momentarily suspended by the love in his eyes. How could she have ever doubted him? She lifted a hand to his face and brushed a wayward lock from his forehead. "In my heart, I knew all along the kind of man you were; I was just too afraid to believe it." She traced his lips with a finger. "But I'm not now."

A very pleased grin slowly spread beneath her fingers. "I assume, then, it's safe to tell you that Angie thanks you for the unscheduled vacation to Winnipeg."

She clasped her hands behind his neck with a sly smile. "Very clever, but can anything outdo the antics of Jake's Corner?"

He chuckled and nibbled her lip. "No, and you're as kooky as the rest of them!"

She tossed her head back, laughing in pure delight. When her eyes returned to his, her whole body went weak. She'd never known the hunger of a man in love.

"We still have one small problem, spanning a few thousand kilometres, Eve," he said, in-between tracing kisses down her neck. "Would Toronto really be so bad?"

"It wasn't Toronto I hated, Dane. It was all the painful memories," Eve said, his breath warming her bare shoulders. "I could live anywhere as long as it's with you, but I don't know if I can simply abandon Jake. I'd need to know he was cared for."

Dane's kisses wandered back up towards her mouth. "We'll just have to see what kind of compromise works best for us, but I promise to do whatever it takes to ensure that you're happy, wherever that might place us."

He captured her lips. There were still so many unanswered questions, so many things to tell each other, but she didn't care. Kissing Dane for the first time without the torment of her past was ecstasy. There would be time for talking later. For the moment, it was time to speak the language of love.

EPILOGUE

Eve climbed the stairs and stopped at the top to catch her breath. These days everything seemed to tire her. She padded down the hall and softly pushed open a door, peeking inside.

Her sons slept soundly. Twins. Two-year-olds. They were tuckered little fellows having spent the day fishing with Daddy and Grandpa Jake. She grinned. It was hard to decide which man was more potty over the boys. They'd be absolute idiots over a girl.

Jacob had kicked off his blankets as usual, so she crept in and tucked them under his little chin. Picking up a teddy bear from where it had fallen to the floor, she lifted Joey's arm and slipped it underneath.

Dane was standing in the doorway, watching her. "How's my angel?" he asked, pulling her close when she came to him.

"Which one?"

"This one," he said, nibbling on her ear.

"Tired today."

"You're not missing the lodge?"

"I haven't had time to," she grinned. "And Andrew's wife is going to do a great job running the place. I feel like I don't have to worry about a thing."

The baby kicked, as it always seemed to whenever Daddy was near. Dane rested a heavy hand on Eve's belly and waited for another kick. He didn't have to wait long.

"What did Gilbert's aunt have to say?"

"She said it's definitely a girl." Eve smiled. "And that if she's right you have to buy Gilbert's boy his first bike."

Dane chuckled. "If she's right, I'll buy Gilbert's girls their first bikes too."

Eve laughed. Jake's Corner teemed with new life and vibrancy. Gilbert had married the daughter of a Caribbean diplomat who had stayed at the lodge during its opening week, and now had two daughters only ten months apart. He was waiting for the birth of his son as eagerly as Dane waited for a daughter.

After a long chase, which everyone for miles around had avidly followed as though it were a soap opera, Stanley finally convinced Crystal Desrosier's cousin, Alice, to marry him. They had no children yet, seemingly content with their new auto repair shop, Alice proving to be a more competent mechanic than Stanley and Gilbert put together.

No new people had settled in the area as yet, but there were jobs, and many businesses which had all but died were thriving once again.

Gilbert was now fully responsible for overseeing the organization of all tours and out-trips, while his young wife helped out whenever she had time away from the babies.

Dane, who had assumed full responsibility of Jake's affairs, had demolished the *Last Chance* and built a smaller, more efficient building in its place, hiring a young local couple to run it. He then built a brand-new home for Eve along the lake, a short distance from the lodge. Given the success of the lodge, he was now considering putting up lodges in other remote communities across the North.

Jake was the only one at Jake's Corner who seemed to be slowing down. Everything he did took longer than it used to, and although that saddened Eve, a light shone in his eyes that she hadn't seen since before Mrs. Jake died, and she knew her family had put it there.

Dane and Jake had become like father and son and Jake had stopped calling him Dang the day the twins were born, although everyone else at Jake's Corner still called him Dan.

Eve smiled up at Dane. She had never dreamed such happiness was possible. "Have you read Nelson's letter?" she asked, referring to the envelope protruding from his shirt pocket.

Dane kissed her cheek and nudged her down the hall towards their bedroom. "Mmm ... hmm."

"What did he want?"

"Newson Enterprises is merging with another company, and he wants me to become an active shareholder again and help with the negotiations."

"And?"

Dane switched on the bedroom light, following her in. "And what?"

"What are you going to do?"

He wrapped his arms around her heavy belly and kissed her neck. "Nelson only thinks he needs me. I'm going to sell him some of my shares so he'll have controlling interest."

She leaned her head towards his kisses which were working their way to her lips. She loved him more with each passing day, placing his happiness above her own. "Dane, if you want to go back to Newson Enterprises, I won't stand in your way," she murmured. "Home is wherever you are."

Dane removed his shirt and turned off the light. Moonlight filtered in through their bedroom window, casting shadows over his chest. He was still as muscular, but they were a working man's muscles instead of a weight lifter's.

Reaching for Eve, he drew her to the window. Looking out over Lake of the Wolves, his arm around her waist, he said softly, "This is my home now, too. I could no more go back to that life than you. I love my family, I love this place ..." He grimaced. "Including sour old Jake, but most of all, Eve, I love you."

Eve leaned against him and stared up at the stars, the contentment in her heart larger than the universe itself.

Dane nibbled her neck. "Well?"

"Well what?"

He bit her earlobe.

"Ouch!"

He bit her again, this time more gently.

"Oh for Pete's sake, Dane! You're a bigger baby than the boys," Eve cried and then laughed. "Dane Newson, I love you."

He grinned. "I don't believe you. Why don't you prove it?"

She laughed again. "Two sons, and now a daughter on the way, doesn't?"

"It's a start."

She lifted her arms to his shoulders; she couldn't reach any farther than that anymore. "I'm unclear on exactly what it is you want. Why don't you show me?"

"I think I will," he murmured, lowering his lips to hers.

ABOUT THE AUTHOR

JORDANNA BOSTON's desire to write was awakened on her first visit to Hawaii. The island's stunning beauty kindled a longing to capture in words what only the heart can express. Besides romance, she loves to write poetry. Jordanna is still looking for Mr. Right (she has the dress, ring, wedding planner etc.) but is just waiting for that last detail - him. She says, until then, there's Ponder Romance.

Don't miss out on the latest news from Ponder Romance!

"Ponderings"

Ponder Romance's biannual newsletter, featuring the newest Ponder Romance, the latest of delightful escapades by the very romantic, Dominick Miserandino, and much more! Complete the reader survey below and we'll put you on our newsletter mailing list!

Please circle the appropriate answer/fill in blanks:

1 Was this the first Ponder Romance you've read? *yes/no*
2. Which novel did you read?..
3 On a scale of 1-5, *(1 poor, 5 excellent)* how would you rate the novel you read? . ...
4 Was there anything in particular you did not enjoy?........................
. ...
5 Was there anything you especially liked?..
.. ..
6. What is your opinion of the cover?...
7. How often do you read romance novels? *regularly, occasionally, rarely*
8 Would you read another Ponder Romance? *yes/no*
9 Where did you obtain this Ponder Romance?......................................
10 Your age *under 18, 18-25, 26-34, 35-50, over 50*

____
Name

____
Address

____
City State/Prov. Country

____
Code

Mail to:

Ponder Publishing Inc.
PO Box 23037, RPO McGillivray
Winnipeg, MB R3T 5S3
Canada

Ponder Publishing Inc.
60 East 42nd Street, Suite 1166
New York, NY 101655
USA